The
Blue
Line

Photography
by
Lewanne
Jones
&
Eric
Goldhagen

The Blue Line

A Novel in 26 Miles

Daniel de Roulet

Translated
by
Paul
Haviland

Autonomedia

Designed
by
Jim
Fleming

Proofread
by
Tanya
Solomon

Original French edition ©1995
Éditions du Seuil, Paris, France

English translation ©2000 Paul Haviland
This edition ©2000 Daniel de Roulet

We gratefully acknowledge financial
assistance in the translation and publication
of this book from Pro Helvetia Foundation
and the New York State Council on the Arts.
Thanks to the New York City Roadrunners
Club and the New York City Public Library
for additional maps and images.

Autonomedia
POB 568 Williamsburgh Station
Brooklyn, New York 11211-0568 USA

Fax: (718) 963-2603
Email: info@autonomedia.org
Website: www.autonomedia.org

Printed in the United States of America

Contents

00   The Verrazano Toll Plaza   09
01   The Verrazano Narrows Bridge   20
02   Exit to 92nd Street   27
03   Fourth Avenue & 83rd Street   33
04   Fourth Avenue & 64th Street   38
05   Fourth Avenue & 44th Street   47
06   Fourth Avenue & 23rd Street   56
07   Fourth Avenue & 3rd Street   61
08   Ashland Place   70
09   Lafayette Avenue   77
10   Lynch Street   83
11   Bedford Avenue   88
12   Manhattan Avenue, Brooklyn   94
13   Pulaski Bridge   103
14   Vernon Boulevard   107
15   Queensboro Bridge   112
16   First Avenue & 59th Street   120
17   First Avenue & 75th Street   127
18   First Avenue & 95th Street   133
19   First Avenue & 115th Street   137
20   Willis Avenue Bridge   146
21   Fifth Avenue & 137th Street   153
22   Fifth Avenue & 120th Street   158
23   Entrance to Central Park   165
24   Central Park & 84th Street   170
25   Central Park & 66th Street   174
26   Central Park & 62nd Street   180

For
Giangiacomo
Feltrinelli

The Blue Line

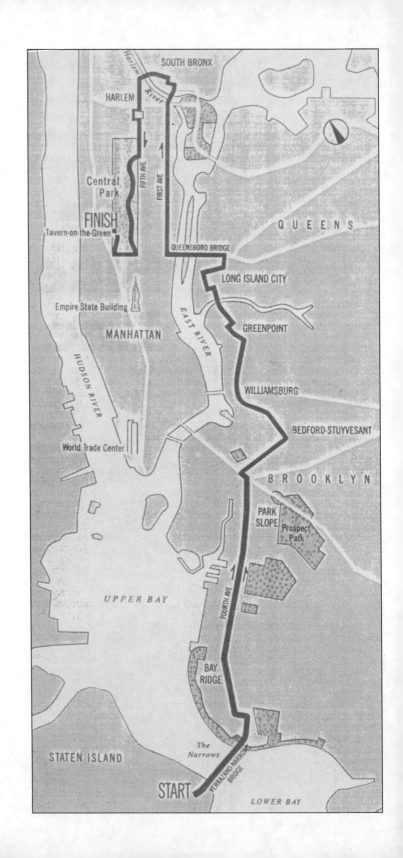

O
THE VERRAZANO TOLL PLAZA

As there was no more suitable place in all Attica for the deployment of cavalry than Marathon, and as it was also very near Eretria, it was to Marathon that Hippias, son of Pisistratus, guided the Persians. Warned of their arrival, the Athenians too set off at full strength to Marathon. [...] Before leaving the city, the Athenian commanders dispatched to Sparta a messenger whose name was Pheidippides, an Athenian and a professional runner. [...] Pheidippides, whom the Athenian commanders had sent to Sparta, and who said that the god Pan had fallen in with him along the way, arrived in Sparta the day after his departure from Athens. [...] The herald delivered his message to the Lacedaemonians, and they were resolved to come to the aid of Athens. [...] The Athenians were unleashed, and they charged the barbarians at a run. There were no less than eight stades between the two armies. When they saw the Athenians running towards them, the Persians made ready to receive them, but observing that the enemy were so few in number and, unsupported by cavalry or archers, were charging on foot in a suicidal attack, they concluded that the Athenians had taken leave of their senses. That was how they assessed the situation; but the Athenians fought them at close quarters and gave a fine account of themselves. As far as we know, this was the first time the Greeks had ever mounted a running assault. [...] The barbarians sailed around Cape Sunium, intending to surprise Athens before its troops had returned. [...] But the Athenians marched with great haste to deliver their city, and arrived there ahead of the barbarians.

Herodotus, *The Histories*

Not many runners have had enough sleep. Here there are no dreams, only the counting of hours. The book says: the final night's sleep is not decisive; you should calculate the average over the last five nights. Max checks the figures again, reaches a total of thirty-five. Seven then. Which will do, in spite of waking this morning after only four hours' sleep. The rest was spent tossing and turning, randomly going over the mob scene at the starting line, some problems at the airport construction site, each refreshment stop in turn, the work schedule for the cargo terminal, his argument with the French woman, the crossing of the Bronx, the finish at Central Park. The book advises: Let your thoughts do the run first. The exercise consists of mentally going through every twist and turn of the course, leaning on the bends, gaining momentum on the slightest downhill, anticipating the moment of discouragement whenever a long straightaway — Brooklyn's Fourth Avenue, say, or First Avenue in Manhattan — suddenly comes into view. Good preparation means never saying I've still got four-fifths ahead of me but rather: The first fifth was a breeze, so the others... Somehow you learn to distract your own thoughts, play a trick on them, but not really by lying to yourself. Max picked that up at a management seminar: The mind latches onto whatever it can. At another, he remembers: God preserve me from moral pain; the other kind I can deal with on my own.

He raises the sash window, using his back muscles, and leans out from the 22nd floor over Park Avenue, now deserted. A discarded cardboard box, flattened over a subway grating, bears testimony to the nightly stalking of the homeless.

Fifty-three degrees Fahrenheit, clear sky — blue even before the November sunrise — a light sea breeze. Ideal weather conditions, according to the forecast on the living-room TV that is never switched off. Probability of precipitation at under five per cent. Conditions are perfect for an attempt on the world record... The Mexican is hotly tipped to win the men's race... In the women's field, a 42-year-old Dublin woman is back in the competition after giving birth to her second child...

Not too much humidity and just cool enough to let the body breathe as the miles add up.

At six-thirty he has breakfast, zaps over to a life insurance commercial, stares through the window at the reflected daylight on the skyscraper opposite. The book advises against any changes in eating habits. He mixes half a yogurt with granola, adds a spoonful of vegetable oil, drinks a coffee and an orange juice. You are what you... There is no one to wait on him. The cleaning lady will come tomorrow and do the week's dishes.

He goes to catch the bus — specially painted in the colors of the Marathon — at the corner of Park Avenue and 87th Street.

1060 Park Avenue. The obsequious doorman, whose cap and livery sport this address, offers a Good morning, sir! tinged with surprise at seeing him so early on a Sunday. On weekdays he sees him leave twice each morning, first with bare legs and running shoes,

then later, from the garage, in a dark suit, at the wheel of a BMW.

The bus is not yet full. Max takes a window seat marked, ironically, NOSMOKING.

At each stop more runners climb on. With a friendly nod in the direction of no one in particular they take their seats in silence. Cradling their sports bags on their laps, they run a last-minute check: shoes, warm clothing for the finish, a fruit juice container or some such amulet, the all-important number bib, a garbage bag to use as a windbreaker, and which will be discarded at the starting line.

At Hudson Dock they pass by a luxury liner bound for Hamburg. On deck, a few passengers are stretching their arms and legs. A silhouette points at Max, who is focusing on his gut. Jitters? Or that orange juice, which tasted odd? Almost as if it had fermented. Take time for a final, relaxed bowel movement, as the book says. Do not change your routine. Which is easy to say, when this first Sunday in November is unlike any other he has known.

The bus glides towards the tunnel that links Battery Park and Brooklyn. Warehouses, docks covered with graffiti, the twin towers of the World Trade Centre all slip by. In front and behind, more buses filled with the same silent athletes converge on the entrance to a hole under the ocean. A group of South Americans, already in a festive mood, noisily offer their friendship but there are no takers. The bus climbs back to sea level and up again to the raised Brooklyn-Queens Expressway. The left-hand lane is already jammed. The passengers indicate with their chins towards the Verrazano-Narrows Bridge looming on the horizon, its cables stretched between two masts, like a giant ship ready to cast off superhuman moorings.

Waiting for the start begins three hours too soon.

At eight-fifteen, the New York City Marathon's official competitors are brought together on the toll plaza, a vast twenty-lane apron leading to the bridge. The Verrazano Narrows have been crucial to the defense of New York over the centuries, as Fort Wadsworth makes plain. Max deciphers the letters, enunciates with difficulty, and repeats: Wadsworth. Once and only once a year, the army opens the base to anyone willing to run twenty-six miles away from it.

Max thanks the bus driver, who wishes him good luck, and gets in line. He shows his number at successive checkpoints manned by grinning volunteers, all yelling benevolently. Several times Max drinks water from the paper cups which are being handed out along the way, and which are beginning to fill the recycling bins a little further on.

Nine o'clock: standing in line at the longest urinal in the world. For more than a quarter mile in the open air, two lines face one another without embarrassment. There are hundreds of portable toilets for the women.

Nine-thirty, back in the same line. It's the nerves. No one pushes; each line is five men deep. Some foreigners remark that the urine is especially light-colored here. I hope they get a picture of this.

The air is still sharply cold, even under the big tents of translucent plastic reeking of all the salves and ointments known to man. Before the warm-up period you wander about aimlessly in this crowd of self-absorbed individuals: Japanese men wearing feminine, see-through silk tights; Scandinavians shielding their bodies with sheets of newspaper, as if they had just joined the ranks of the homeless; women unabashedly changing their bras; Hindus cloaked in garbage bags, deep in med-

itation; a native American reading the *Wall Street Journal*.

At ten o'clock, the buses at the other end of the fort open their doors. Each runner deposits a bag of clothing that will be waiting at the finish, arranged by last name and in alphabetical order. Max drops his at the letter M. That leaves only the long sweater that goes down to his knees.

Fifty thousand thighs, calves and ankles are now ready to be warmed up. Jog, bend, concentrate, relax. Max lies down on a piece of cardboard, creating an inviolable space around him. No one takes any notice of him. It's everyone for himself, and the race is open to everyone. He closes his eyes; believes he is opening wide his unconscious; relaxes all his facial muscles, his limbs, his navel. His body becomes a motionless hollow tube through which air flows unceasingly, and withdraws into the serenity of a flattened encephalogram. Max contemplates the little lapping waves of his childhood, painted by Courbet on a bend of the river Loue; hears the wind rustling in the hazel trees; recites, in the characteristic accent of the Jura, Mon pays de juments indomptées, indomptables: my country of untamed, untamable mares... His eyes open after five minutes' sleep, and he stretches every muscle he knows of. His head is empty, but not his bladder. Once again, he goes to line up.

Over the loudspeakers someone is explaining how this great herd is to be let out of the pasture. Runners wearing numbers preceded by an X are to proceed to the tollbooth at the far end, where they will be admitted to the starting area. They fling their last articles of warm clothing onto the leafless branches of nearby trees. Jeans, bright new sweatshirts, barely-used scarves, old headgear, last year's polychrome jackets: all are sacrificed on these Christmas trees for the homeless, to whom the clothes will be given during the day. At $20 per item, there must be half a million dollars left behind. The crowd is growing happily excited, stamping like a team of mares at the stable door. Max's number, now visible, is checked one last time. He is left with a pair of nylon shorts, an army singlet, a headband, white silk gloves and a small electronic device, an insignificant weight to carry.

He heads towards Verrazano Toll Plaza along with others who have stated on their enrollment forms that they intend to finish the race in four hours. Nine minutes per mile, including refreshment stops, disruptions at the start, other halts dictated by physiological needs. The goal, for a first marathon, is relatively ambitious. He has, for the time being, replaced it with the desire merely to finish alive — and to make an end to this footrace that, since the beginning of the year, has had him rising early to the surprise of his doorman and of all the doormen in the world.

The actual starting line is still a few hundred yards away. The runners are bunched ever more closely together; there is hardly room to tie your shoelaces.

In the tense moments before the starting gun, the runners can see that they are generally taller than average, and thinner than average. Their faces are more emaciated, more sharply lined. A few couples have entered. Others hear familiar accents, and become superficially acquainted, inquiring: Is it your first?, or replying, with the benefit of previous experience, You'll see, the public carries you right along. All are prey to irrational doubts over their equipment — what if it rains? — and their fluid intake — if one paper cup contains two measures, how much do two and a half cups contain? — and the conditioning of their muscles, now wrapped in gooseflesh.

An Italian asks Max how many marathons he's run. "None, I've never been in a race." The Italian invokes the name of the mother of Christ in his own language and adds, "I hope you're not over fifty!" Max makes no reply, although, yes, he is... but only just.

The countdown has begun. Not so much the massed ranks of Athenian warriors, without armor, at Marathon — naked before Hippias's horsemen — but more a mass demonstration poised to cross the bridge into the city, which they will seize and conquer as free agents. They stand erect. No one will order them to crouch behind the starting line as was the custom in those ridiculous marathons at the beginning of the century, with their trappings of military discipline.

There is a sense of fraternity, of belonging to a chosen group, in the dense starting pack. The street has been occupied; the forces of law and order have retreated, outnumbered.

On the order of His Honor the Mayor, a dull boom resounds from the cannon on top of Fort Wadsworth and unties the knot in each stomach. The roar of the crowd blows away any last-minute butterflies. Those in front have broken away while the rest jog impatiently on the spot. Max reaches the actual starting line after four and a half minutes, which he will deduct from his personal time. He joins half the participants on the open-air upper deck of the bridge, while the other half take the lower deck.

Thousands of air-cushioned, gel-cushioned and foam-cushioned running shoes fly forward across the Verrazano Narrows. The Statue of Liberty is not yet in view, hidden among the suspension cables that support the roadway. Max went up there once, into her crown; he can see her now, to his left, nearly behind him — but it is only a glimpse, the crowd has him in its surge. Yet in that glimpse he notices that Liberty's head is at the same height above sea level as his own feet. Immigrants arriving early this century would have seen her from below as they stood on deck and the boats came into port. *Amerika*, page one: The arm with the sword rose up as if newly stretched aloft, and round the figure blew the free winds of heaven. But the sword that Kafka saw was only a torch, and liberty a tiny island.

Ellis Island — an immigration center, then a McCarthyite prison — is rather larger. There is an island for every dream in America, all the way to Honolulu.

Fireboats spraying great arcs of colored water salute the start of the race with all sirens blaring, like toys floating in the bath of the god who watches over runners. Helicopters, hanging in mid-air on some celestial thread, hover at the same height as the frontrunners: the god Pan again. Sixty-odd bumblebees packed with teams of cameramen behind each glass eye, feeding down to some 6,000 accredited journalists.

The bridge rises imperceptibly to 300 feet above sea level, the highest point in the race; the view is not unlike that studied by the passenger as the plane circles in a holding pattern. We apologize for the delay in landing, which is due to temporary air traffic congestion...

In 1524 Giovanni da Verrazano, a Venetian, became the first European to reach the bay, at a time when Manhattan meant hilly island. The Verrazano Narrows Bridge is the world's longest: two and a half miles. Designed by Amman for cars only, it was opened in 1964. It has been the sole preserve of pedestrians for one day a year since 1977 — on condition that they run.

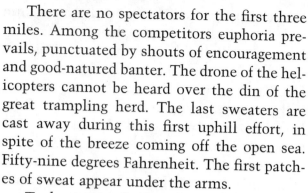

There are no spectators for the first three miles. Among the competitors euphoria prevails, punctuated by shouts of encouragement and good-natured banter. The drone of the helicopters cannot be heard over the din of the great trampling herd. The last sweaters are cast away during this first uphill effort, in spite of the breeze coming off the open sea. Fifty-nine degrees Fahrenheit. The first patches of sweat appear under the arms.

Tugboats can be heard tooting now and again as the wind shifts. Spouting fountains of green, yellow and blue, they are floats in a parade fit for the nation's heroes, home from Normandy or Saigon, or from some Gulf war. The production is pure Hollywood, and is being broadcast live by twenty television channels at least.

Max picks out the point ahead at which the overhead cables begin to curve upwards again. This perception is more mental than physical; the impending descent has not yet been registered by the legs. On the left, Liberty now reveals herself above the bridge parapet, at last disentangled from the mesh of cables. Behind her, further up the Hudson, lies an unreachable island, a prison where enemies of the dominant lobby end up. For crimes both common and political.

To his right stretches the Atlantic, and below that horizon lie the lands where the boat people, the migrants, begin their journey. Places like Max's Jura: his Europe.

* * *

The loudspeaker in the station at Olten announced: "Now arriving at platform three, the 7:09 service from Milan, bound for Frankfurt. Carrozza di prima classe, settore B." His berth had been reserved for the whole of the journey from Italy, and his ticket was valid as far as Mannheim.

His night run was over. It had taken five hours from the Rhine, crossing four villages and the town in the valley, over snow, over the crest of the Jura, then racing back down again.

He rubbed his sore thighs and read the passing advertising slogans, written in some muddled language: CIGARES MECARILLOS... BIÈRE FELDSCHÖSSEN... He bought a can of beer and a small pack of cigarillos from the sandwich vendor as he worked his way down the aisle, ignored the no smoking sign and drank an early morning toast to the health of the lobby.

He broke the trail en route to Germany by going down to Basel, then changed trains and headed towards France. At the first stop after the border he got off and recovered his car.

His hands tensed at the wheel when the 8 o'clock news bulletin reported the first details of his anonymous act. By ten he had arrived at work in Ornans. He was freshly shaven, unnoticed, unnoticeable.

The 8 o'clock evening news on television featured a government minister, one of the lobby's hostages, deploring the events of the night before.

The next day's front pages revealed the time — almost down to the minute — he had begun his race. His private marathon: private, yet meant for the public, although he had run it alone — unknown. With no one on the sidelines to cheer him on.

For a few days his namelessness was on everyone's lips.

1

THE VERRAZANO NARROWS BRIDGE

For years people were literally paralyzed by the legend of Pheidippides, the runner at Marathon, whose task was to deliver news of the Greek victory over the Persians. He set off on a wild and dramatic dash to Athens, some fifty kilometers from the village of Marathon.

Pheidippides uttered a single cry: "Victory!" Then he collapsed, struck down by exhaustion. Tired to death, literally. And for a long time those who dared to run the marathon were thought to be crazy. Until the day Emil Zátopek, the famed "Czechoslovakian locomotive", broke into a smile as he crossed the finish line of the London and Helsinki marathons.

Cordner Nelson, *Advanced Running Book*

The downhill, now discernible, becomes more pronounced. As they pass the east pylon on the Brooklyn side, some raise their eyes to the reinforced concrete summit where the cables are anchored. Journalists with telephoto lenses have made it their perch and are capturing the familiar souvenir shot of an army of ants on the move, evenly spaced and all heading the same way.

The caravan is still compact as it gathers speed on the downward slope. Different muscles come into play. Max lets the natural momentum propel him forwards.

A snapshot from October 23rd, 1977, shows the bridge with a mere 5,000 competitors — a world record at the time. No need for both decks of the roadway; just half the lanes on the upper, open deck accommodate all the runners. Bill Rodgers, wearing the number three, leads from the start. The basic outfit hasn't changed much. The cut of the shorts, the neckline of the singlet and the treads in the soles of the shoes have undergone minor but costly style changes. The difference between New York's first marathon and this one lies elsewhere. Today's runners are electronically equipped. The smart watch on your wrist displays local and international time, measures tenths of seconds since the start, calculates average speeds, monitors your pulse and the number of strides taken, wakes you up... or alerts you with a beep that the split time you've set yourself for the completion of a mile will soon be up. Your flight plan is pre-programmed, leaving the automatic pilot free to direct the pace. Next, the headband, incorporating your choice of ultra-lightweight devices. It may accommodate a walkman, a minidisc player, a radio that you can hook up to your own private transmitter. You activate these headband functions from your wrist. No wires are needed. Turn up the volume on the headphones tucked into the headband; tune to a different radio station; stop. Silence for a few unplugged minutes.

True fanatics have a miniature camera on their wrist and video their own faces at various stages of the contest.

Real pros (those now nearing the exit from the suspended bridge) do not transport a single gram needlessly. A watch is the only accessory they take on board. The gadget-laden are, in fact, a small minority. Running has become the last line of defense against sports equipment overload — no comparison with the cyclists and skiers shackled to a thousand trademarks. And why would you want to fill your ears with waves plucked out of the ether, when the breeze makes such uncommon music from the cables of the bridge? When the foghorns fade in and out as the wind turns, and you catch the rustling of conversations above the still smooth rumble of so many footfalls?

The bridge looks as if it is ready to set sail with its crew of twenty-five thousand sailors, its steel cable riggings stretching up to the foremast, photographers keeping lookout from the crow's nest. "Cast off!" cries Hippias... Some Persian ships manage to get away from Marathon; the others are left behind to burn.

On Max's wrist is a device with two buttons. One controls the chronometer, the other dials up his home phone. This allows him to record his observations along the way. In his everyday life Max carries a notebook in which he is always jotting down a note, a reminder; since he cannot do so now, he has provided for an oral history to be chronicled. A few short remarks at each mile, so he can reconstruct the whole course. His answering machine at home will take the message each time he has something of interest to report; the microphone is concealed in the wristband. Maintaining the pendulum swing of his shoulders, Max presses his right thumb to his left wrist as he goes past the second pylon of the bridge, counts ten strides while the answerphone plays the outgoing message, "This is Max... I'll get back to you as soon as I can". He can hear his own voice under the headband. He brings the wristband to his mouth and reads out the traffic signs overhead:

BROOKLYN EXIT LEFT   **TRUCK ROUTE EXIT RIGHT**

Pressing once more with his right thumb, he concludes the recording. One memory, freshly minted.

Pheidippides encountered the god Pan on his way to Sparta; the runner may experience a moment of illumination. The book calls it runner's high, and notes that it can occur after several hours — or at any time. You can't predict when or where. Max hopes to preserve that moment on tape.

* * *

He finally reached Olten, the endpoint of his forty-two kilometer race. He felt no exhilaration.

He retrieved the baggage reclaim key from its hiding place behind the balustrade of the famous wooden bridge in the old town. In the station toilets, he again changed clothes. Not out of fear of detection by the forensic squad, since his face remained undisguised, but because wearing a sweat-drenched shirt on such a cold morning was to invite pneumonia. He adjusted his tie and, in lieu of a shower, applied a dash of cologne from a sample sachet he had kept for that purpose. He threw his wet clothes into a rubbish bin that would be emptied during the day, taking no particular precautions as he did so. He only left the toilets once the train had pulled into the station, aiming for the briefest possible exposure to the random curiosity of strangers.

Departure for Frankfurt at 7:09 a.m.

* * *

The Italian runner who had called upon the Virgin at the start of the race has reached the downhill section of the Verrazano Bridge. He catches Max's eye, gives him a friendly wave

and points him out to his two compatriots. They in turn shout a few words of encouragement in the language of Gianni Agnelli, then go back to concentrating on their socks, immaculately white and banded just under the knee with the national tricolor. Max smiles at them, thankful for this temporary bearing in a sea of anonymity, and, focusing on their somewhat overdeveloped calves — perhaps they play soccer — strives to keep in synch. Their stride is smooth, feet skimming the ground with minimum lift, palms turned downwards, torsos straight and shoulders relaxed. Max asks them if they train together, as it's unusual to see three techniques so similar side by side. They seem to move at the same well-measured pace; they don't understand his English.

A short, stocky man with very white hair has been tailing Max for a while. They smile and the old man points to his number. "Our numbers are in sequence," he says. Max replies that they are determined by alphabetical order. "No, it's by order of picking up your number," says the old man. Max tries to remember if he saw him last Wednesday at the center where all the runners had to go to pick up their number cards and other paraphernalia — a souvenir vest, a fannypack full of free samples of shaving cream, soaps and washing powder, a baseball cap, sunglasses, a poster suitable for framing, and a raft of brochures for all the upcoming marathons: in Fukuoka this winter, Paris in springtime, Stockholm and Prague next summer, San Francisco in the fall. Then in the hemisphere of opposite seasons: Rio, Melbourne and Johannesburg.

Max sizes up the old man and reckons that his legs must have run thousands of miles, but he replies, "No, just like you it's my first time". He's sixty-one. Any other sports? "Yeah, I swim, I was once on the Irish national team." But why does he run? "My daughter died in a highway accident this summer. I can't seem to get over it."

Max says nothing. He feels a lump in his throat, though his pace is unaffected. Can't think of a response. The old man looks very fit; he's got the bull-neck of a swimmer, muscles with plenty of flesh on them — no sharp angles — and creased eyes, as if they were trying, but failing, to weep. He says that after the race he's going to Florida to tell his aged mother that her granddaughter has died. Then he moves on to the weather in New York and how lucky they are.

He is running for his daughter. Others do it for money: the mercenaries. They were the first ones to get away at the start. They will take two hours and ten minutes to finish, and burn off no more calories than those who take four. They can win $60,000, a luxury German car donated by a local dealer, and three days of being talked about. A Zulu runner from South Africa tells the press that the prize money would equal thirty years' wages for him. People recognize him at the training sessions. He signs autographs; the logo of a footwear manufacturer looms behind. While the average participant only has to fight off periodic bouts of low self-esteem, these professionals have real opponents — though they may claim to be uninterested in any lane apart from their own: I do my running entirely within a four-foot-wide track. They affect indifference to both rankings and cash. But should their shadow be overtaken by a competitor's shoulder, their loser's tears will show them up cruelly.

The women are a more agreeable sort. They make up only a quarter of the total, are ranked separately, and are applauded with genuine warmth. There are men as old as eighty, whereas women over fifty are quite rare, having only recently been declared eligible for the longest distances. Yet the woman setting the pace today is forty-two years old — too old for a man to expect to win. To the dumbfounded press pack she declared: "Fortunately I don't have to worry about getting my period!"

The old man is a pro. Even when he changes disciplines, discipline is what he knows. He trains by swimming two lengths underwater. He knows that every contest has a nervous beginning and a serene aftermath. Athletic competition is as routine for him as recitals are to a musician. He may be initially gripped by stage fright, but the minute he makes his entrance he lets himself go, trusting in reflexes acquired through long practice. Whereas, for Max, in his first public race, there are no precedents.

The Verrazano downhill is not very steep, just enough to let you change pace. From that point on, you find your own. Finally you have room for your feet, for your elbows, for your shoulders.

The approach ramp, its degree of curvature designed with the turning angle of automobiles in mind, sweeps down to terra firma. Now the marathon pours onto it; in a moment the attacking Athenians, with cries of Charge!, will spill from this massive pontoon and make landfall in Brooklyn.

2
EXIT TO 92nd STREET

The Directoire systematically went about organizing footraces, which would embody the democratic values that needed to be disseminated. On August 10th, 1796, races were held throughout the country to commemorate the fall of the throne. On such occasions the event conformed to a standard type. The rules for the race on the Champ de Mars, as published on July 22nd, 1798, by the Interior Ministry, stipulated that squads of fifteen men should be formed, and that one after the other each squad would start from a gate near the Thermes towards the goal placed in front of the altar of the homeland. The winners of each heat received a feather to put in their hats and returned to the start to take part in the final. The prize awarded to the three fastest runners (certified by a judging panel of schoolteachers) was a saber or a pistol.

Gérard Bruand,
Anthropologie du geste sportif

The banner over their heads reads WELCOME TO BROOKLYN! Those who have run the first three miles on the lower deck emerge to find a clear blue sky as they merge with the pack from the upper deck, who have come down on a tighter bend designed to make up the difference in distance between the two starting routes. The caravan bunches up again on the first left turn. Here is where the real contest begins: each stride counts, each foot glides even closer to the surface. As the crew disembark from the Good Ship Verrazano they

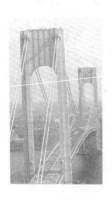

encounter the first spectator, followed immediately by thousands of others. Balancing on the highway divider, leaning out of windows and peering over rooftops, they cheer the runners on with total sincerity. The less likely they are to be capable of running — if only across the road — the louder they bellow, peppering their encouragement with good-natured scolding or ironic threats:

"A big guy like you, come on!"

"Hey, number X18976! Step on the gas!"

"You in the red shoes and the white headband — you're gonna wish you hadn't!"

These personalized messages are the joyous, spontaneous offer of assistance from the onlooker to the runner whose pace may be dragging a little. A woman in pink, briskly applauded, returns the compliment with a knowing smile. By word and gesture it is implied that we're old friends, that this is the very place we've agreed to meet — here in this forgettable corner of a foul suburb where even the R train doesn't go.

Apart from the odd graduation ceremony or conference presentation, Max has never been publicly applauded in his life. Surely all these people are deceived; they seem to think he's an athlete, or someone similar. Ladies and gentlemen, we have a case of mistaken identity.

Running on the weekend, running at dawn, running at night. You have to earn the right to run. Most of these competitors (apart from the retired and the few who are front-runners by profession) spend their lives earning a living. You can hardly afford the $100 fee required to enter the marathon if you haven't got a roof over your head.

But Max is an architect. Airport cargo terminals are his specialty. Each project he directs for his firm lasts for five years; he's presently on his fourth. O'Hare in Chicago,

Schipol in Amsterdam, Abdelzek in Dubai. And now Nagasaki. Besides his job as Head of Cargo Projects, there are invitations to join international design competitions, conferences to attend, clients to visit, board members to report to. Max knows his way around the planet as well as any tour operator. Name a capital city and Max can tell you how long it takes to get from downtown to the airport, or where the Hilton and the nightlife are; the name of the river, or of the main shopping area; the dollar exchange rate of the local currency; the time zone, plus or minus GMT; the average seasonal temperature and humidity; tipping guidelines; the color of the licence plates. At any rate, this is as much as he reveals of himself when a colleague asks him how Stockholm compares to Oslo or whether Seoul is anything like Bamako. Just occasionally he may mention a personal recollection, a smell, a chance conversation, a sweet moment of solitude. It's not much. Does he know that?

Ever since he decided to run, he has been training in the early morning, stepping out of all the hotels in the world, jogging along an Asian coastal road, around warehouses, towards some African shantytown, on an empty stretch of beach outside Dublin, under Parisian bridges where lost youth has driven the vagrants. Of these morning sorties he has spoken to no one. No one is interested in Max outside of work: not his firm, not his women (who see it as time robbed from them), not his doorman. Max tends his private garden, where lowly tubers or succulent passion fruit might grow.

As a career man, he delivers the goods, and then some. According to the professional journals, he marries the simplicity of overall horizontality to the transparent density of tangential superstructures. Not just post-modern, he

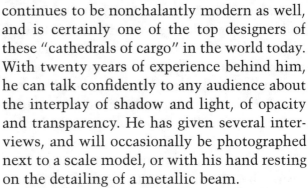

continues to be nonchalantly modern as well, and is certainly one of the top designers of these "cathedrals of cargo" in the world today. With twenty years of experience behind him, he can talk confidently to any audience about the interplay of shadow and light, of opacity and transparency. He has given several interviews, and will occasionally be photographed next to a scale model, or with his hand resting on the detailing of a metallic beam.

When he recruits a new architect for the Cargo Division, he will question the candidate on topics of a purely professional nature, while studying the portfolio of sketches. And as the young man speaks, Max studies the hollow of his cheeks, the posture of his upper torso, the position of his hands — is this a person capable of nurturing a private garden? He fires off one final question: Do you have other interests in life? If the answer is yes, the job is offered. Masks tend to prefer masks.

The marathon goes through the five boroughs of New York City, starting at Staten Island, then Brooklyn, Queens, the Bronx and Manhattan. As the course hops from one island to another, it crosses five bridges.

Brooklyn: from the Dutch Breuckelen, a village near Utrecht. At the turn of the century, those immigrants still in Manhattan but still in poverty were deported there en masse, compelled by simple economic pressure. So it is that, since 1910, the population of Manhattan (which had then peaked at two and a half million) has been declining at about the same rate as Brooklyn's has been rising. The building of bridges over the East River simplified the process of sending workers from their jobs in the skyscrapers to their beds in Brooklyn. There are not many who, like Max, both live and work in the fashionable city center. Every evening Manhattan's tunnels and bridges spit out a million and a half commuters.

The marathoners disembark to the sound of applause in the westernmost corner of Brooklyn, a suburban neighborhood of low-rise housing where the living is apparently not easy. The first storefront on the course, at the corner of Hamilton Parkway and 94th Street, belongs to Perry's Gunshop. The caravan now doubles back on itself; its head can see its comet's tail stretching back to the giant cause-way suspended 300 feet in the air. On the rut-ted pavement a dotted blue line (repainted only the week before) slips between two tight-ly-packed rows of onlookers. It marks out the shortest route, taking every corner and bend as tightly as possible; end to end, it measures twenty-six-point-two miles precisely. Now it veers right, up a slight hill, along 94th, then right again, into Fourth Avenue. Ahead, a maple tree still shedding its red leaves and the Nagasaki, a Japanese restaurant.

Branching off at right angles to the blue line, all the way down Fourth Avenue in Brooklyn, are about a hundred streets; the dis-tance is five miles. The line is not (as the map seems to indicate) wholly straight and flat. So as not to give discouragement a foothold, it is careful to bend slightly with each variation of the social strata. It weaves its way from Lutheran to Latin American, from legal to ille-gal immigration, visiting a pocket of Irish here and an enclave of Greeks there. It even drops in on a few white Anglo-Saxon Protestants: dentists and gynecologists.

At each intersection, for the record, Max reads out the words on a sign or billboard at eye-level. After the beep, he brings his left wrist up to his lips and speaks into the micro-phone, down the phone line to his answering machine:

94th Street	Nagasaki Restaurant
93rd	Domino's Pizza
92nd	Animal Hospital
91st	La Magnifique 2
90th	Carmen, Nails & Skin Care
89th	Food & More
88th	Ponte Vecchio
87th	Hellas America
86th	Liberty Fax Service
85th	Unisex Alexandria
84th	Joel L. Sokol, D.M.D. Dentist

* * *

The city of Olten, dentists included, was still asleep before seven. Near the hospital, a newspaper vendor was spreading salt over the icy sidewalk. He had already changed the flier on his stand. Referendum — the people's verdict. A close call for the lobby.

The Circolo Italiano was brewing up coffee for Turkish workers, smoke on their breath even before the first cigarette. Cars, wary of black ice, proceeded with care, white beams lighting up residual patches of slush.

He crossed a public garden where for several years a man — a native of these parts, his arms all knotted muscle — has been trying unsuccessfully to free himself from a block of granite, that symbol of the permanence of the Confederal State. He turned right onto the bridge, threw his gloves into the water, and entered the train station through an underground passage. Advertising posters promised NATIONAL INSURANCE, or INSURANCE UNION, or HOUSEHOLD INSURANCE, as if there were nothing else on which to build a country in the middle of the world.

3
FOURTH AVENUE
AND 83RD STREET

Sixty thousand pairs of eyes strained to identify
the leader as he entered the stadium. It was
number seventeen — Louis! Pandemonium
broke out, and men and women wept openly as
the little shepherd trotted wearily towards the
finish, dwarfed by the lanky Prince George of
Greece, who had leapt from the royal box to run
with Louis over part of the last lap.

Tom McNab, *Flanagan's Run*

Now, at last, the race has attracted the audience it deserves. Two and a half million spectators, not to mention millions of TV viewers.

A rock band is playing on a flatbed truck. They've borrowed the carport roof of a local garage to stack their amps on. In black leather and shades, moving jerkily to the beat, they are paying proletarian tribute to the middle classes now streaming by. They'll get their photo in the paper tomorrow; someone will make a note; they'll be offered a gig outside Brooklyn. The runners respond with their own whoops of appreciation. In the crowd, a ripple of applause for the guitar solo.

Volunteers, all smiles and good cheer, are out in force. Some are ex-runners; most are dedicated fans whose weight, age or inability

to make time for training means a walk-on part, proffering water, blankets and constant shouts of "Go for it!". They'll come away with a T-shirt ambiguously proclaiming that they, too, took part in the marathon. They are the race's helping hands. There are thirteen thousand of them.

Max spots a group of Spartans discussing — in French — the International Breakfast Run, a three-mile race that brings the marathoners together on the morning before the main event. As the flags of all nations flutter over UN Plaza, speeches ring out in all languages, extolling cooperation in sport and the right of international intervention; in any case, may the best man win. As this propaganda for the Marathon Way of Life drones on from overhead loudspeakers, the runners are compiling and comparing evidence of social standing. Despite the presence of an authentic proletarian from Greenland (his trip sponsored by an entire village), this is an upper-middle-class crowd whose luggage flies business, not charter, and whose track suits are of the latest generation of man-made fiber. For them, a watch is a fashion statement and a scent must be discreet. They are tanned, but not from working in the fields. Gone are the lean years when a free meal and a winner's purse were enough to lure the jobless of the Midwest into the hands of shady promoters staging fights and marathons. The social ladder has been turned upside down: affluent competitors now pay for the privilege of joining in the ordeal. The only debts they have to worry about are for that second, extravagant car.

After the speechmaking, the Breakfast Run. Some fifteen thousand runners jog through central Manhattan, taking in Madison, Park and 6th Avenues, to the finish line in Central Park. There, in a secular communion of souls pretending (for a time) to believe that the body can move faster than the mind, a light breakfast is served.

Coming up to 83rd Street, Max overhears the French contingent recalling yesterday's event. They have nothing but admiration for the organizational skills of les Américains. "Fantastic the way they do these things here, no pushing and shoving. In France, if there's so much as a line for the ski lift, you have to bring in riot police just to keep things civil..."

One of them — his accent is uptight Parisian, inflected with the expectation of privilege — goes further. "We're in a place where people actually trust democracy."

"And do it with a smile," adds the trailing Frenchman, who's level with Max. Who adds nothing.

Yes, this is the middle class, with every reason to be smug. Yet its representatives are here today because, in a departure from the day-to-day, they have challenged themselves to twenty-six miles. To within an inch of their abilities. And that is what, at the Breakfast in Central Park, accounts for the discreet charm of, you know...

Anyway, the ones who finish are no longer who they were when they started. Why should Max turn his irony on them?

Max jogs along a street in Athens, having had a few hours of fitful sleep and a quick coffee in a still sleepy square some miles from the Hilton. He's attempting to work out how that first marathon runner, the shepherd, fought off heatstroke on this uphill stretch. A hard, hard run in midsummer. From the top, the sea below is violet and the tumuli — mounds of bones, of Persian warriors in their thousands, beneath the dry grass — are yellow. Did he savor the downsweeping view?

What kind of footwear would a Greek shepherd have had? His mother and his aunts are still here, in that doorway, still in black, sweeping up the leaves that fell last night among the red and mauve petals.

Max calls out to one old woman: "Kali mera!" She stops to watch him for a moment, then lets loose with a stream of incomprehensible words. He smiles sheepishly, wipes away the beads of sweat ganging up on his eyes. ...No wristwatch on that shepherd's arm, of course, but what soles on his feet?

His prize, as winner, was a lifetime of free shaves. Heroes have no further use for a beard.

The blue line's memory runs on all the while, and Max enters some more data in his electronic record:

83rd	M. Vahdad M.D.P.C. Adult Allergy
82nd	Parking lot, locked at night
81st	Every Child Needs A Jewish Education
80th	Lutheran Church
79th	Colonial Apartment
78th	Jovin C. Lombardo M.D.
	James J. Lombardo M.D.
	John W. Lombardo M.D.
77th	The United Korean Church of New York
76th	Masonic club
	Bay Ridge Luxury Co-ops
74th	Medical Imaging Mammography
73rd	S. Mariae Angelorum Dicatum
72nd	Comprehensive Podiatry
Lovington Ave.	Methodist Church
Bay Ridge Ave.	Te Amo, Imported Cigars
68th	Diagnostic Analysis
Senator St.	Tonino's Pizza Inc.
67th	Building Schools For A Better Tomorrow
66th	Pizza Gelato
65th	Free 492-0824
64th	Amoco Full Serve, and a car full of cops

The sign, on the outskirts of Olten, read
POLICE — 1400 meters. By now, an all-points
alert must be flashing on every desk in every
cop station, so it would be inadvisable to
saunter past, under their very noses. But he
liked a bit of provocation, especially if it
involved a game of chance. He proceeded
down the snowbanked road, an ordinary jogger
out for his morning run. A No. 2 bus pulled
up. Color: orange. Make: Berna. For a ticket
from the machine, he'd need change, but all
he had was a 20-franc bill, his emergency war
chest. The driver could prove helpful, but
might recognize him later from photographs.
He trotted on down the main street, past a
man in a tracksuit — no athlete, clearly —
whose immaculately groomed basset hound
was emptying its bladder. Further on, he
encountered a morning fitness fanatic, who
waved at him. Max followed suit, adding a
friendly but inscrutable grunt that acknowl-
edged local affinity while maintaining a certain anonymity. He kept his eye, though, on
the ominous light in the police station.

Just as he passed in front of it, the door
opened. Out came two tired uniforms. Night
shift was over.

4

FOURTH AVENUE AND 64th STREET

The marathon took place on July 19th, 1900, a few days before the end of the Olympics. The race began on a 500-meter oval track that belonged to the Racing Club de France in the Bois de Boulogne. The course then wound through the streets of Paris before returning to the oval track. It measured 40.26 kilometers. This Tour de Paris proved too much of an ordeal for most runners and only eight finished the course. The temperature in the streets reached 102º Fahrenheit (39º Centigrade) and no refreshment was provided along the way. The winner was Michel Theato of France in 2:59′45″.

D. Martin, R. Gynn, *The Marathon Footrace*

Block by block, the neighborhoods are getting poorer. Light blue flags emblazoned with New York's apple have been waving from the tops of lampposts for the past week; tomorrow, Monday, they'll be sold off. Everything has its price in the USA, from the logo on the number bib to the post-race interview rights, from the name on a cap to the mention of a soft drink. If you can produce your Official Marathon Runner's ID, you can claim a discount; if you win the marathon, you can claim a luxury car. The organizers do everything except run Max's race for him.

A small Methodist church marks 4th Avenue's high point. Built in 1895, it is a marriage of brownstone and another freestone, with chocolate-colored joins. A large clock-face tells the time, but Max trusts only his watch and his flight plan. He's allowed nine minutes per mile, which, multiplied by twenty-six-point-two, makes — nine times two, eighteen, so a hundred and eighty; nine times six, fifty-four. Total, two hundred and thirty-four. Four hours are two hundred and forty minutes. Constant mental recalculation. He lost four minutes thirty seconds at the start. If he finishes in Central Park...

For the time being, he records the changing context, a Latino neighborhood with plunging property values:

63rd	Home Economics
62nd	Video Liquor
61st	Los Compadres, open 24 hours
60th	H. L. Rappaport Plumbing Supplies
59th	Subway station, El Gran Castillo, Tacos
58th	Irish coffee
57th	Exodus treatment center
56th	Miracles Gift Shop
55th	Superior Market
54th	Comidas Latinas
53rd	Iglesia de Dios Pentecostal
52nd	Ortiz Funeral Home
51st	Consolidated Oil
50th	Clean up after your dog – $100 fine
49th	Mayflower Cleaners
48th	King's Wok Chinese Food
47th	Carlos Hardware
46th	Nadja's Video
45th	Subway station, Jugos Naturales

A blue line of paint down the middle of the street, with breaks at two-foot intervals. Three inches wide, more than a million long. Repainted annually, a few days before the marathon, its length is guaranteed accurate by means of a bicycle-wheel odometer. The req-

uisite 4,219,500 centimeters are not always measured down the middle of the pavement, but stretched as tightly as possible against any curve, hugging every bend to allow absolute economy of effort. At such points the blue line may come to within five feet of the sidewalk. As it does so, it preserves the rounded trajectory of the human body in motion, leaning naturally into a turn. The line's taut contour represents the shortest distance between the starting and finishing points.

Once the early crush has dispersed, the blue line reappears from under feet and legs and becomes the sole guide, while subjective time advances in irregular bursts. Each new mile is signaled by a flag of contrasting color, visible from afar. The line regulates the positioning of water stations, toilet facilities and supplies of sponsored food. Its shade of blue recalls the shutters on Greek houses in Attica, where flies never settle. It is the azure of the sky at dawn over Nagasaki, or of the underside of an olive branch that the wind has exposed, just outside Athens; it is the blue of Max's great-uncle's eyes; it is the horizon behind the Chrysler Building, as painted by Courbet from the Brooklyn Bridge. You cannot go wrong. You follow it to the end.

Neither boundary line nor line of fire, it does not bear the name of a general or the number of a degree of latitude. It is not the craggy skyline of the Vosges, birthplace of Jules Ferry. It has a beginning and an end, like a book within which Max would enclose his whole life.

He is learning the knack of naming it in even breaths. At cruising speed it is three puffs out for each intake, counting: the...blue...line. On the fourth beat, he breathes in, as if the final E were pronounced and aspirated: "the, blue, line, ah..." Four strides exactly, then start over, each time on the same foot. A chant he must repeat more than 14,000 times, at least in thought (subtitling the film: Marathon!) before the blue line comes to an end.

Max carries his mirror with him, like Saint-Réal walking his reflections down a country road in The Red and the Black and creating a novel out of them.

"Life is a road movie," Max tells his mother, who has come over from Europe (only for his sake, she says). She stays at a luxury hotel, speaks of his elder brother, implicitly chiding: "At least he keeps up with the family." Is Max beholden to these people? At fifteen, perhaps. But at twenty, or forty? And now, at fifty?

Even before finishing high school he was in line for his uncle's manufacturing business. There is a sumptuous property on the banks of the Loue — a stone's throw from the cemetary painted by Gustave Courbet — with every comfort and convenience, including a tennis court. His uncle calls the chauffeur Max, distinguishing the young heir as Mr. Max. This produces the following exchange:

"Hi, Max."

"Good morning, Mr. Max."

He has a teenager's loathing of class distinctions and decides to change his name. No need, they send him away to school in Switzerland.

He will emerge from the Federal Institute of Technology in Zurich with a diploma in architecture and a paternal offer (because he is smarter than his elder brother) to take charge of a Bolivian subsidiary and reorganize the local market in construction materials, asbestos and cement. But in the room where he lives and studies, Che Guevara watches over those who would betray the people's cause. A poster printed in Italy by Feltrinelli.

Max agrees to fly to La Paz. Friends of the family will welcome him with a dinner party, where all will be revealed of certain tactical alliances with certain bloodthirsty generals. At the poolside, he will note the unbearable lightness of being rich and observe the pathology of their wives, their pawns.

No thank you, he won't be having any.

Revolted, back in Ornans he throws himself (with all the background intelligence at his disposal) into the war against the establishment's order. He takes up a job in Germany with a major corporation whose construction sites disfigure the whole planet.

He phones his mother once a month, but otherwise makes no concession to the clan. One sister, depressive, still living with the parents; one brother, a predator, now recycling his capital into the cement industries of Eastern Europe, where the family originated. One father, the exemplar, elected to the Senate in order that the will of finance should be done, even unto Parliament.

Newspaper photos of his father amid the ranks of government officials, he fears, send an ambiguous message. He can hardly hide his origins, given such physical resemblance: the same lean profile, the same little fold over the left eye, the same hands and overlong fingers. The same scornful turn of the head, mocking an adversary.

Over the past decade, Max's rise through company ranks has been effortless — almost unwilling. Yet his estrangement from his White Russian family is common knowledge, as is his militant past and questionable ideological commitment to the market economy. Yet the detachment he brings to his work earns him the esteem of his colleagues and superiors. Never getting involved in power struggles, unburdened by territorial ambitions, he is valued for what the company terms his input on cultural and human resources issues. He seems to have no attachment other than his attaché case. He is as free as the free market, yet never attends the firm's many social events.

His present posting is at Head Office (Worldwide) in Manhattan, where he is Head of Cargo Terminals. From the top of a skyscraper he coordinates air terminal construction sites across the globe in order that merchandise should move and its rule prevail, now and to kingdom come.

His secretaries and co-workers would say: Max works like a fiend. He's from a good family, but seems to have broken all ties. Never has anyone over. No heartaches... no kids. You've got to admire the way he keeps his private life private. An image of perfect smoothness.

The last time he saw his father was five years ago in Frankfurt, on his birthday. The patriarch was coming expressly from Franche-Comté for a man-to-man talk. It would take place at the airport, in a private meeting room with a view of the western runway, where goons of the regime once clashed with defenders of the forest.

His father seems tired. By saying tired, it is possible not to think old.

For years now, silence has filled the infinite space between them. There is body language whereby the elbow declares, the back exclaims, the rib cage interrogates: with such a grammar, communication is established. Even without signifiers, people signify. Except, for Max, in the case of his father. One's being-in-the-world excludes the other.

A heavy fog has settled inside the room where they are to hold their conversation. Words are exchanged — words like the

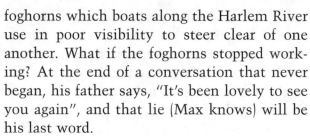

foghorns which boats along the Harlem River use in poor visibility to steer clear of one another. What if the foghorns stopped working? At the end of a conversation that never began, his father says, "It's been lovely to see you again", and that lie (Max knows) will be his last word.

Max's generation took up Gide's cry of Family, I hate you without ever really burning their bridges. As family members grew older, the dubious compromise would persist — a few more phone calls, a slightly longer visit to an ageing eccentric uncle. Whispers in a hospital corridor as illness ushers in woe.

One day, like his father now, Max will stop running. In the meantime, he will not be compared to those aimless crowds cheering for someone else's endurance.

In the firm's landscaped offices, next to the glass-fronted conference room by the mail desk, photocopier and coffee machine, a poster urges him to sign up for the marathon. His fellow workers are surprised when he asks about it. They only know what they've heard on TV. In their presence he feels neither young nor old, but overeager. They have no strength left for new departures; they are too busy consolidating, too afraid to emerge from their bunkers. They are married to their jobs, just as surely they are wedded to their mothers-in-law. Of all this, Max knows only the single life.

He decides to sign up, one day in the middle of a work session in Nagasaki. Plans for the new air cargo terminal are spread out on the table. A colleague leans too far over; his shirt splits, revealing an ugly flab characteristic of the male who no longer looks after himself. Through the window, the mimosa lining the driveway fence is in flower. Max makes an excuse, goes out for fresh air. And takes a decision. He no longer wishes to belong to their world. He wants to keep his distance. Tomorrow he'll start training.

A week later, during a conference on civil aviation and its hangars in Athens, he asks a taxi driver to take him along the historic course that begins on the plain of Marathon and cuts right across the northern suburbs.

The city seen from above.

* * *

The mountains rose up from the Rhine; in successive folds, they formed two terraces dotted with villages and separated by the valley and its chief town. The Jura range swept in from very low and climbed gradually to the high ridge, from whose crest, on a clear day, you had a fine view of the plain and, beyond that, the Alps.

He was admiring the lights of the town below, in the plain which they call a plateau. The way down would be steep and short — under three kilometers to Olten railway station. He could have launched himself on a hang-glider from here, high above the outskirts of the city, and landed next to the tracks.

He spared his aching limbs from any movement that was not strictly necessary, and they gave thanks for it.

A bus was scheduled for five past six, just in case his own legs could not rescue him. He would rather not take the risk of being seen, since it was all going so well. He continued down the hill towards the first dwellings. The Romans built this road through the col to reach their camp at Augst, and it was on this venerable highway, half snow-covered between two chalky walls, that he now disposed of the last pieces of evidence. Having

45

already burned his clothes more than twenty kilometers back, he would now do the same to the map (drawn to a scale of 1:50000) on which they could find his fingerprints and the thin line of pencil that traced his steps that night. He lit the fire.

Nothing now differentiated him from the ordinary citizen out to greet the dawn. On the brow of a small hill on the plateau, he could see the antenna, its red light winking right at him: the police's radio link with their colleagues in other provinces. He sent his own smoke signal in reply, sticking out his tongue at the antenna. The flame barely warmed his gloves.

He scattered the ashes, then fairly flew down the hill.

5
FOURTH AVENUE
AND 44th STREET

In the Roman heat of September 10th, 1960,
Abebe Bikila of Ethiopia is running. Sweating.
Thirsty. To win, they've told him again and
again, he must avoid drinking, so he does not
drink. His toes bleed over the rough ground. He
breaks away from the pack and takes the lead.
The race officials are wondering where this
complete newcomer, who runs barefoot, could
have come from. Suddenly he is caught by the
Moroccan, Rhadi, who passes him — and spits
in his face. Abebe Bikila controls himself; better
yet, he puts on a burst of speed, leaving Rhadi
behind. Abebe wins the gold medal with a time
of 2:15'16".

Serge Bressan, *Les Marathons*

A yellow flag at the intersection with 44th
Street alerts you from a long way off to
the tables on either side of the pavement.
Rows of paper cups have been set up, each
containing water or an isotonic drink. For the
sake of a few seconds, some runners will skip
this one, but the book advises against it for
those trying their first four-hour marathon. It
also warns you about the threat of slipping on
discarded cups. Take your time, sip rather
than gulp, keep running in place. Even slight
dehydration may cause a significant drop in

performance levels. As it is written, so shall it be drunk.

Each runner has his own band of supporters in the crowd, with whom a given signal and specific location have been agreed. The office turns out in force with a banner: GO JOHN GO! A child's voice: C'mon dad! Some woman: I love you, John!

Max is expecting no one. His elderly American uncle, a "character" whom he occasionally takes to Saturday brunch, has no interest in sports. Indeed, he has no interest in anything. The woman he thinks of as the French woman is at home. As for the Italian woman, she's out of the country.

At each new intersection with Fourth Avenue the street number decreases by one. This countdown is heartening, for they will all have to be passed by on the way to Third Street, mile seven of the course. In front of Max is a black man straight out of a bodybuilder magazine. His muscles glisten with sweat: enormous biceps, monstrous quads. Impressive, although the book makes it clear that, when it comes to running the marathon, each unnecessary ounce of muscle is deadweight.

Max has lost sight of the old man running for his daughter, so he concentrates on the bodybuilder in his gleaming white gear advertising United Color of B. Letting yourself be paced by someone else helps your rhythm as well as your state of mind. Each stride is easy.

For the second time the course goes under a highway. (The first one, back at 65th Street, was Interstate 278.) The overpass is painted green on rust; a pulsating echo resounds underneath. Max dials his answering machine to record the party atmosphere, boosted by a live band playing Lou Reed's "Halloween Parade" at full volume. A worthy addition to the soundtrack of his memories. He overdubs a title and commentary with a tap of the finger.

Back in the open, the blue line looks like a single unbroken stripe for the first time. Thousands of runners can revel in their own image, repeated endlessly as far as the eye can see, right up to the dogleg where Fourth Avenue skirts around the Williamsburg Savings Bank, whose age and size make it Brooklyn's most esteemed skyscraper.

The black man glistens more than ever, but his pace is becoming less reliable. Now a college girl (her T-shirt declares she's in love with John) moves past the bodybuilder, whose pumping fists rise higher towards his chest with each new stroke — a bad sign. The ratio between muscle mass to be shifted and the work rate those same muscles can sustain is changing for the worse. White running shoes against black skin begin to wobble ever so slightly; the cardiac pump is too small to do the job efficiently. Max too passes him, looks back, looks into bulging eyes that will give out in the next few yards. Frantic eyes, shot with distress: staring at defeat, if not intensive care. Max's race has hardly begun. He could give the poor guy some encouraging sign — just a nod of solidarity — but you don't run for the others. It's between you and yourself, between Max and himself, between Max and Max.

Pump up your muscles and that's what happens: your body is no longer your own.

He's watched them, in the torture-chamber gyms of big hotels right across the planet, lifting chrome-plated weights a great deal heavier than their brains, gasping on running machines as the speed inexorably mounts, simulating a skier's angle of attack, eyes glued to the action video on the screen as biceps, triceps and quadriceps tan and swell. Adding volume, like a hairdresser, from an aerosol can.

Max treats his body with moderation. When he subjects it to a sauna or a cold shower, he feels no compulsion to display, or savor, the pain.

To avoid the fate of the deflating hormone-filled muscleman, you have to build more than your body, and not conspire against it — since, as everyone knows, your body will get you back in the end.

44th	Launderette
43rd	Concerned Citizens Of Sunset Park
42nd	Good American Food
41st	America Market
40th	Rose Unisex Salon
39th	Merit Cigarettes
38th	Bush Terminal Associates
37th	vacant lot
36th	dogs and security guards
35th	Florist, Funeral Designs
34th	Pork Products
33rd	illegible graffiti
32nd	Turquoise Nite Club

Max's cleaner comes from around here, on 32nd Street. Once a week she cleans his apartment and throws out the toothbrushes that occasional women have left behind. She calls him the bachelor.

Perhaps he has a type. Skin color: varies from the luminous white of a Japanese woman to the very pale white of a German. He would say that he shows them all the same respect.

He is the friend and lover of a few women.

At times he has been confronted by the other's desire to bear his child, whereupon negotiations open. The drama then unfolds in regular episodes on and around the futon, until the final abortion — never undertaken lightheartedly.

The last time, with the French woman, she had even named the child. The matter has left its mark, a memory somewhere between them yet beyond their control.

The other evening, as they were walking down Lexington Avenue, she brought the whole thing up again, even having the nerve to say she wanted to start over, and this time we keep it. But the opposite of hope is not despair; it is Max's lucidity when it comes to love. He has never been around children. It's just not his style, can't you see?

As for the Italian woman, he finds her perfectly straightforward, which may be a fault. From head to toe, taking in all the rest: her belly, her flattened navel, her black bras, her perfume and her smile, seen from below as she leans over him, tongue out for him. Crying out between taut lips. He can see all the joins, on every part of her, even in her soul.

Occasionally she will break off in the middle of a laugh, plunge her dark eyes into Max's, and — moving away — demand a genuine vow. Max dodges: you know as well as I do... Or, why do you think you need to hear those words?... They're just words...

Max loans himself to many, gives himself to none. Not even to...

DANIEL DE ROULET

La Ligne bleue

ROMAN

ÉDITIONS DU SEUIL

He uses the so-called Progressive Marathon Training method, which he got from a book. In three parts: before, during and after. Twenty-six-point-two miles in four hours. You don't get there in one go. You start with ten minutes, then twenty. Then an hour, every day at dawn, when the New York air is still sharp. After six months you're up to two hours at weekends, and three weeks after that you begin extending it further. By June, Max had reached three hours.

By the end of July, it was three hours and twenty minutes.

By the end of August, three hours thirty minutes, but he has to stop several times during the last half hour.

Mid-September: another stab at three and a half, but he keeps hitting the same barrier: the Wall, as described in the book. Cold sweats, breathlessness, severe hunger pangs in spite of the glucose intake. The body plunders its last reserves.

During that last half hour, Max cannot stay in stride for more than two hundred yards. It's as if he were the runner breaking the tape in a slow-motion replay. Calf muscles in spasm, thighs heavy as blocks of granite, excruciating pains in the soles of his feet. Even the gentle swing of the arms is agony. Max's book says the important thing is to keep going, no matter what. What it doesn't describe is how hard it is to come home and drag yourself to the bathtub, incapable of doing the slightest stretching exercise. What's the point?

Then there's his stomach, which won't take anything solid afterwards. It seizes up with cramps for two days before eventually settling down.

At the end of September, the vagaries of air cargo terminal standardization find him in a four-star hotel in Paris. He decides to try for the full four hours and plots out a twenty-five mile course that will take him along the Seine.

Sunday dawns with ideal conditions: a light, cool wind and no sun. He does the first hour as if he'd set out to do five. Stops at a fire hydrant spurting water and drinks the quart of liquid he's already lost. At the end of the second hour, when he should have reached the halfway point — the return ought to take as long as the outbound journey — he finds he's two miles short, through an error of scale on the map no doubt, or his own failure to take account of elevations, the odd footbridge or lack of a sidewalk. He stops at a public fountain in some gray suburb, fills up, and starts to head back. All goes well for the next half hour. Steady rate of respiration. Easy, clean strides. No stitch in his side, no fog on his glasses — an indication of excessive perspiration, at least in cold weather. No stiffness in his neck.

Then comes a long straight down the narrow bank of a still deserted highway, and here discouragement sets in. Something to do with the monotony of the scene, probably. As long as the environment keeps changing, he can concentrate on whatever is new, but a straight that is too straight can sap his morale utterly.

He has to pull up. After that, he cannot even find first gear. He shuffles onward towards the horizon, towards Bercy and its warehouses, envying the ability of everyone in the world to accelerate past him. Several attempts to restart the engine fail miserably: the tank is dry, the cartridge empty, all your troops have been routed. You're a pedestrian now. The sidewalk ahead. The sounds of bicycle bells and car horns. A woman with a shopping cart trying to get past him — Pardon, Monsieur! — she's in a rush. This never happens — to be aware that others besides himself are in motion.

But the wings on his heels, in this nightmare, have fallen limp and the messenger of the gods has come down to earth. The serpent and Icarus and Max, their feathers burnt on the sun of speed.

Nothing wrong with his heart rate, and no particular injury — not even a blister, or a nobler muscle strain. No, it's a comprehensive exhaustion. His inner pilot, located somewhere between brain and stomach, has become disconnected, out of reach. Willpower is not at home, leave a message. Physiology up against the wall.

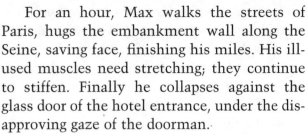

For an hour, Max walks the streets of Paris, hugs the embankment wall along the Seine, saving face, finishing his miles. His ill-used muscles need stretching; they continue to stiffen. Finally he collapses against the glass door of the hotel entrance, under the disapproving gaze of the doorman.

It is not momentary fatigue that inspires dread, but that great immobility, always circling. The one that pins old folks to their armchairs before finally settling on their lungs. So he runs, hoping to speed past it, since he can't trip it up. What do you find on the other side of the wall, beyond the twenty-mile mark: ecstasy? Or death? The book only deals with the obstacle itself, and he has just taken it right on the chin.

Would this failure pass? Could it be permanent? In his hotel room, Max watches the night close in. Desolation.

On the last page of his diary, Charles-Ferdinand Ramuz has written of the hour of the sick and dying... As shadows take over the room, you cannot catch your breath... You are divested of your self.

* * *

He was on the last uphill stretch. Like the Jura, he had climbed from the banks of the Rhine, first in a gentle sweep up to a shelf of flat land, then down to the town in the valley, snugly enclosed on all sides; then higher still, onto the second shelf, where a string of villages and isolated farms slumbered; and now he was climbing again, up to the ridge crest. From there, the city of Olten would be visible below.

All was silent as the grave.

The col was a long, tedious one, but its strategic importance to their army was manifest. The pass would be secured from the huge trapezoidal parallelepipeds, painted in camouflage, that lined the route, while sunken yellow lozenges on the road surface indicated the positioning of anti-tank defenses. Thus would they repel the invading (yellow?) hordes poised to sweep across their independent mountains.

The road was too exposed to be wholly reassuring to anyone hoping to avoid detection at the close of a winter's night, miles from any respectable dwelling. True, there was a parking area for Sunday drivers and three restaurants, all closed. But there could be no logical justification for anyone to be here at this time. If a car stopped to offer him a lift, say, he would spin some tale about an army induction course involving a hike. In this part of the country it would seem natural to be on a military "mission" — as natural as collecting coins in a Yuletide kettle for that other army, the one that calls itself Salvation, outside a department store.

No sound of vehicles, however, emerged from the darkness. He was breathing faster and as silently as possible as he passed the restaurants. No barking dogs, no light apart from a perpetual neon glow at the gas station. A layer of snow had accumulated on the plastic cover of a car (the owner's, no doubt) in front of the gas station. Between now and the end of winter...

6

FOURTH AVENUE AND 23rd STREET

A strange fate awaited all three Tokyo medal-
ists. Tsuburaya resumed training with the 1968
Mexico City games in his sights, but an
Achilles tendon injury, along with persistent
stomach pains, hindered his preparation. After
his defeat in Tokyo, these new problems over-
whelmed him, and so, in the traditional
Japanese way, he committed hara-kiri.
Basil Heatley suffered a particularly severe case
of heatstroke only weeks after taking the silver
in Japan, and retired from athletics for good.
Abebe Bikila, who had torn a knee ligament
before the Mexico games, knew that a third
Olympic victory was beyond his grasp. He abandoned after seventeen kilometers, handing the
gold to fellow Ethiopian Mamo Wolde. A few
months later, Bikila was in a car accident that
left him in a wheelchair for the rest of his days.
He died in 1973.

Alain Lunzenfichter, *Le Marathon dans la
foulée du professeur Saillant*

So, twenty-five thousand: the number of
runners the bridge can hold at the start of
the race, perhaps, or the number of medals the
factory can turn out. There could even be a
mathematical model (expressed as a curve) to
demonstrate that, past a certain point, volunteers will outnumber the participants.
Twenty-five thousand, then: fifteen thousand
Americans, drawn by lot from the pool of

sixty thousand who put in for a number. Fewer foreigners apply, so they stand a better chance of being accepted.

There are one hundred spectators per runner. There could hardly be a single one who, tomorrow, would recognize Max in the street, stop to say: well done. At the moment, however, they are lavishing personalized tributes on him. An old man waving his cane shouts, Can I have your legs when you've finished? In Europe, the cheering is monosyllabic, meaningless.

At the corner of 21st, an intellectual tries to dart across the street with his Sunday *New York Times*, weighing about two pounds, under his arm. Beaten back by the unyielding onward rush, he retreats to the sidelines until the anti-intellectual current has abated somewhat.

For his next recording, Max presses the button on his wrist with his thumb, preparing (as ever) to mentally count the ten beeps before the machine answers, but the line is busy. Someone else is calling him.

Ahead on the sidewalk a little girl, all dressed up, is stretching out her hand to him; he obliges with a high-five, palm against palm.

"Go, go!"

The girl turns delightedly to her dad, a large man also in his Sunday best.

Something has gone wrong. No one except Max can leave a message on his machine. He programmed it himself last night to divert any incoming calls. He punches the button twice, as if to punish the faulty electronics, which now produce a screech followed by two clicks. The tape rewinds to the outgoing message; he should be able to record now. Suddenly there is a woman's voice in his headset.

"So, Max, you're running the marathon."

This produces a disturbance in his pace and heart rate; his breaths come after two strides

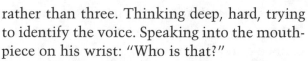

rather than three. Thinking deep, hard, trying to identify the voice. Speaking into the mouthpiece on his wrist: "Who is that?"

"You remember me. It's Ingeborg." She was known to everyone as l'Allemande: the German woman. She is there, her voice in his head.

Grasping for something to say. Goes back to three breaths out for each breath in, but words do not come. Max dislikes an uninvited audience.

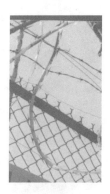

Memories of his life prior to emigration catch him out at odd times, in unexpected places — a hotel room, or at work, huddled over blueprints for an airport, or (naturally) while running.

How could she have caught up with him now? True, he'd phoned her the last time he was in Nagasaki. But how has she managed to reach him via the answering machine? Max speaks into the mouthpiece on his wristband: "Where are you?"

Dead air. He double-clicks to reset the machine, waits for the tape to rewind, repeats his question. The tape is rolling, ready to record. Gone, this mysterious momentary scare. Into thin air.

It was a classic piece of staging by the German woman, with her fondness for surprise appearances and cybergadgetry. Telecommunications — the extensions of man and his planet — were the Trojan horse that allowed her to infiltrate virtual reality. He occasionally heard from her by e-mail. But in fifteen years he had not set eyes on her.

* * *

Their first meeting was over tulips in an airport.

Ingeborg had gone through passport control on the wrong side. (Excess of caution, failure to communicate.) They caught sight of one another through the glass barrier which was also a border. After some pleading with customs officials, they were allowed to kiss, once and for all. A romantic scene to bolster the latest theories of incommunicability: the body's language of love behind air terminal glass.

She traveled frequently for her work, and often departed for good. Sometimes she went away for reasons that could not be discussed, and which Max did not wish to know anyway. Her two passports, the blonde wig or surgical gloves in her purse did not perplex him. Over the course of their hotel-room relationship, he had discovered that her violin case, where she pretended to hide a supply of sanitary napkins, also concealed passport photos, rubber stamps, rosin (but not for the missing bow) and a number of electronic devices.

So: no innuendoes, no inferences, but discretion and modesty above all else. How often they would meet was penciled in elsewhere, by others. She was as independent as he; never once did she condescend to the vocabulary of lies in the language of passion. It was a kind of self-control. Ingeborg's lips were sealed by her secret society.

* * *

The Jura did not stretch from the banks of the Rhine to its full height in one even sweep. A gradual slope led to the first village, then there was a bowl, at the opposite end of which lay the town. Beyond that, a narrow plateau held the second, third and fourth villages. Then a further climb to the top of the ridge. The final rise before the crest itself was almost sheer.

For some time now he had kept to the road — always a risk — but at this point his map

indicated a steeper alternative. He could cut straight across a hairpin bend and come out at a point on the road that would give him a better view of the terrain ahead. But the map did not lie: its contour lines promised an arduous climb, more easily negotiated on paper (or at least by day) than by night, in winter.

He climbed like an animal, on all fours, so that he always had three grips. Hanging on through the white cotton gloves that he would jettison when crossing the river, just before taking the train. The fear of a false move made him tighten a bit. In his pocket he carried a strong painkiller that might help him escape — with a broken leg, for instance — the dank prisons of this land.

He grunted softly as he climbed, all the while commiserating with himself, for he had no one with whom to share this fear in his belly.

He managed to keep his balance — straightened himself, then grew more confident. He was grunting a little still, but (with not a soul to commiserate) now hurried on his way, as silent as he could be. On the outside. He wasn't so accomplished at the inner silence yet.

7
FOURTH AVENUE AND THIRD STREET

In 1984 women were allowed to compete in the marathon for the first time. Late on Sunday morning, August 5th, 80,000 spectators packed into the Los Angeles Coliseum witnessed the plight of the Swiss runner, Gabriella Andersen-Schiess. Suffering from heatstroke, severely dehydrated, she looked like a disjointed rag doll as she ran in. Officials shadowed her every step but did not intervene, and she finished under her own steam, risking her life there on the track.

R. Parienté, G. Lagorce, *La Fabuleuse Histoire des Jeux olympiques*

The blue line now traverses a territory from which houses, even sidewalks, have been erased. First the buildings burned, then their insides were gutted; walls crumbled, then collapsed. Finally the rubble would be bulldozed away. Weeds grow tall behind the chain-link fences topped with barbed wire that keep the car cemeteries, cardboard cities and marauding troupes of teenagers at bay. Bleak tracts of no-man's-land that will continue to lie barren until property values revive and a profit can be creamed off by the corporations of Manhattan, in whose vaults the title deeds are safely cocooned.

An exception has been made for city-owned land, some of which is now given over to community gardening by local people who have organized, occupied and won the right to farm the urban jungle. At the corner of a street whose name has gone missing, a sign on the fence thanks the Mayor of New York and his deputy (and his deputy's deputy) for their participation.

Further along, the waste ground has become a public dump, as pestilent as any in the third world; later, there are lots filled with second-hand cars bound for auction. Any walls still standing are covered with graffiti, up to impressively acrobatic heights.

Property values evidently recover as the blue line approaches the Williamsburg Savings Bank tower. A few of the holes in the urban fabric have been patched up. On the gabled façade of one building is an already faded mural, eight stories tall, of the Statue of Liberty embracing a panoramic America of happy black children on their way to school, hard-working Latinos proud to be factory workers, a tall Amerindian looking out into the distant horizon — the excluded, their dream of belonging. A woman crushes a syringe; a Christ-like Malcolm X returns to his people, the poor. And Marlon Brando plays Christopher Columbus.

A black runner — who must have a slight hip disability, he runs with a limp — slows to a stop and takes a picture of the mural for his scrapbook with a tiny camera he wears around his neck.

At the corner of Bergen Street, Max observes a couple (he looks Greek, she must be Italian) drinking beer wrapped in a brown paper bag and mocking the runners who are visibly nearest exhaustion. Max makes out a single jeering word, masochists.

Having decided to run the marathon before he was fifty, Max knew he would need to regain control over his body parts. One by one, he would reassemble them to create a runner — a new self, a seamless identity. From top to toe.

It would need training, every day, from six to seven, Monday to Friday. With a longer run on Saturday or Sunday.

Feet first: the book explains pronation and supination. The former exercises the inside of the sole, the latter strengthens the outside. Shoes next: look for the correct shape, the right degree of firmness, comfortable but secure lacing. Max would add that colour is a consideration, as he dislikes gaudy ornamentation. Up to now he has only worn out one pair, whose left toe gave out long before the three thousand miles guaranteed by the shoestore salesman. This provided an opportunity for Max to perform an autopsy on his shoes, to determine which parts had — despite the emulsion-filled cushions in the soles — proved least resistant to the demands of his own particular anatomy. In the end, he replaced them with an Olympic brand he'd seen advertised in every hotel on the planet.

Raw toes, sore heels and callused sides ensued nonetheless, but Max took daily care of his feet, as the book recommends. They had become the best-maintained part of him, apart from his head.

Between foot and shoe a sock must go. Max's woolen socks are hand-sewn, obtained for him by a friend of his uncle's at the charity bazaars of her local parish. He has also tried white tennis socks and the ones that, for twice the price, feature a reinforced heel and no stitching. But damp cotton begins to grate after two hours of running. Max turns the woolen socks down over his shoes so that they won't bunch up inside them; this also allows direct ventilation of the ankles.

Then, in ascending order, the calves (including a varicose vein on the right leg, inherited from his father) and the knees, with their delicate cartilage, so hard to replace once it's gone. Knee cartilage is the reason you need shock absorbers under the soles of your feet.

One day before dawn, in a London park next to a royal palace where the guard against the Irish was already on patrol, Max felt a dry, cracking pain: a dislocated knee. He stopped dead, the dread cascading through him in the space of a hundredth of a second: it's all over, I can forget the marathon. That much seemed certain. But the setback was only temporary. Fifteen minutes later, nature had restored all the faulty components to their proper settings.

Thighs are more robust, with their unremarkable muscle structure. No particular problem there, as far up as the muscles and bones of the hip region, though Max could list a variety of pains, ranging from dull throb to sharp stab, in a number of places. The body must have an intrinsic need to suffer from time to time, as an affirmation of its very existence.

The male genitalia contract during this kind of exercise, much as they do after prolonged exposure to sea water or low temperatures. They become small, insignificant.

Hips are overtly rebellious subjects. It has happened that, after only a half an hour, Max's hips have simply gone on strike. This in turn corrupts the entire organism, whose performance is subject to the law of minimum effort for maximum efficiency. On such occasions there is no alternative but to resume the posture of the primitive biped, slouching towards a taxi and a long soak.

Consider the torso: the mechanical side of things here is far from straightforward, with the digestive apparatus running above, along-side and below the respiratory cavities. A cramp on the right side may point to the liver, while on the left it has no specific correlation. Max finds it hard to make sense of, or restore order to, this region. The best he can come up with to remedy its shortcomings is to urge it on with a general, uplifting mental pep-talk.

As an autonomous materialist, Max knows the soul has no seat, but melancholy must be located somewhere in this vicinity.

To the heart — the easiest zone to patrol. Inside the book's covers (edged in red) are instructions on how to take your pulse at the end of training, and five minutes after that. Max even went to the heart specialist and pedaled the bicycle that prints out the graph. Systole, diastole, all clear. You've got nothing to worry about...

Arms: keep them bent. Palms down — when they begin to reach upwards, it's a sign that a sub-system somewhere is beginning to drag the rest of the system down to exhaustion and apathy.

Shoulders can become stiff, gripping the neck in a vise that prevents it from pivoting: consciously relax them on every downhill, before the accumulated strain becomes unbearable.

Finally, the head. It is not the pilot's cockpit. It is little more than a calculator you've brought along to check your running speed by dividing the number of miles covered by the time elapsed. It can't make Max run unless the rest of Max, from head to foot, decides to.

Max has built up an awareness of all these different parts of himself over the miles and by way of sundry recitations and revisitations, things seen or said before. Max invents nothing new as he runs. He conjugates each element of his identity in turn, pulling together the scattered threads of his being-in-the-world. Like all happy post-modern heroes, his one deep fear is to be dispossessed of himself.

On his hands are white silk gloves from Paragon, at the corner of 18th and Broadway. A gift from the French woman.

* * *

Ingeborg used to be secretary of Greenwar, the ecology movement, and lived in an urban women's commune in Germany. Max had gone there to visit a friend of his who was out at the time. Ingeborg was alone, pacing the oversize living room. She'd come down with the flu. Max offered to go out for her. He returned with vitamins, newspapers and a flat square box from the local Italian. They finished their pizza at exactly the same moment, mouths full, eyes locked together. The scene was set for Max's first lesson in aromatic ethnology.

In those days of activism it didn't take long to get down to basics. They had already dressed by the time Max's friend got back. Eros, revolution and the rest.

Their meeting three weeks later at an airport was eagerly awaited by both. She wore a white sweater, no bra (page one, chapter one, Our Bodies, Ourselves), not a skirt but jeans, not heels but white basketball shoes. Even with the plate glass between them in the customs hall, their impatience was noticeable. It became more palpable yet in the car, driving along the river, looking for a parking space. In the elevator they could no longer hold back. A perfunctory tour of the apartment dispensed with, the German woman threw her bag down and closed the curtains. Love at first sight, over and over.

Her visit lasted longer than planned, as did their lovemaking and their happiness: children were even mentioned. She recited haiku to him, taught him the basics of raw fish. Sashimi and sushi you.

By day, Max had his office. Evenings they spent together wherever the movement came together: at the communal center, in various squats, or at the factory gates, during that first egalitarian strike. Among exiles, students, young workers. The seasons changed, twice. Their happiness never did.

Once, she pressed her mouth to his ear (it was during a stand-off with a mobile police unit, their wicker shields against the setting sun), her eyes narrowing, almost closed in ecstasy, and said: That's it, I'm pregnant, I'll be leaving. It was part of the zeitgeist. No attachments. Freed of their fathers, children would not grow up to replicate the family. They decided on a genderless name, Mirafiori, in honor of the Fiat workers in Turin who chanted We want it all! Then they separated.

There would be long letters that spoke of the struggle against the lobby, against the profiteers, the final struggle. Only in the postscript was there room for words of tenderness. Hope to see you again...

* * *

Behind him, four villages, the valley, the town. Ahead, only the col and the sharp descent to the city of Olten. As he followed the winding road, he tried to avoid getting caught in the headlights of passing cars.

Fortunately, he heard the danger approaching: the distinctive sound of a Fiat gearshift. Turning around, he saw the sweep of its headlights through the trees below. He decided to leave the road, cutting across the next bend and scrabbling up the steep wooded slope. He would escape detection with little time lost. But the

diversion cost him considerable effort: the terrain was tricky, the change of pace unhelpful.

He was glad to get back to the paved road. Still, it was hard going, keeping the uphill momentum with a compact stride that made excessive demands on his back thigh muscles.

After the Fiat there was calm, then total silence.

Each breath came from deep down in his lungs. He could not help breathing through his mouth, which meant that the cold now penetrated into his chest. He was wheezing, nearing the point at which the oxygen supply could no longer sustain the impetus. The last reserves of energy would soon be depleted. He visited the furthest frozen reaches of his body, but each stride still felt more laborious than the last. Fists clenched: If I stop now, I won't be able to start again.

On the col looming before him he detected a faint yellowish glow. It grew clearer, seeming to come in bursts. An orange glow now: a revolving light on a vehicle. Max strained to see better, jogging warily towards it. Two white headlights appeared under the flashing light. It was making slow progress. The cops were taking their time; it was the time of day, anyway, when only dawn was expected. They would draw the noose around him on this, his final climb. He looked back, expecting to find himself already surrounded, a piece of light weaponry aimed squarely at him.

His knees would buckle any second now. The three points of light were coming down the pass, seeking him. He ran on. He might as well face this head on, head high, guilty as charged — not shot in the back like a coward.

He strained to make out the sound of the engine over the wind, which was blowing in the wrong direction, and his own hoarse breathing. Would it be a Volvo, meaning the

Zurich police, or an Alfa Romeo (from Solothurn), or a BMW (Aargau)? If they had spotted him, the dogs would already have been unleashed, so he dropped his arms down close to his thighs. They trained their wretched creatures to fasten on to any projecting length of forearm. But he kept on running.

The vehicle continued down the pass, its three beams illuminating the empty road ahead. Two more curves and he would be in the firing line. He imagined the news flash: An intensive police search led to the arrest less than four hours after the incident... Reports say the suspect is a Frenchman from a well-to-do family who...

Last bend before the orange beam.

The revolving light was mounted on a small flatbed truck. At the back, two men in hooded jackets were pouring salt and gravel into a spreader that spat the mixture out onto the icy road surface.

He crouched down in a hollow, concentrating on every sound made by the road maintenance crew as they passed by on their early morning detail. Finally the sound was gone, swallowed up into the stunned silence below.

8
ASHLAND PLACE

At the 1992 Barcelona Olympics, 22-year-old Hwang Young Cho of Korea finished first with a time of 2:13'23", ahead of Koichi Morichita of Japan. In the grandstand was another Korean, Soh Kee Chung, 80, for whom this was sweet revenge. In 1936 he won the Berlin marathon, but had been forced to run under a Japanese name and as part of the national team of Japan, which was then occupying his country.

Young Hwang wanted to do a victory lap with the Korean flag, but he collapsed face down on the track, wracked by cramps and vomiting. Hwang's mother, a pearl diver, is accustomed to staying under water for several minutes at a time, which might explain her son's performance. [...]

Four of the first five across the finish line had to be removed on stretchers. Lamothe of Haiti suffered such violent spasms that he was taken into intensive care.

New York Times, August 10th, 1992

Beneath the Williamsburg tower, four avenues intersect with Fourth Avenue. The blue line angles off to the left at 120 degrees, onto Flatbush Avenue, but only for a few yards.

Flatbush, like Broadway in Manhattan, is an interminable diagonal cut through the right-angled grid of Brooklyn. On any other day of the week, the free nourishment on offer outside the city welfare center would come in the shape of food parcels for the unemployed.

Now the blue streak veers right onto Lafayette, hugging the bend as closely as possible, yet without a fraction's deviation in width.

The Williamsburg Savings Bank was to be the hub of a new financial district that was never built because of the Depression, and with Wall Street being so close by. Halsey's 1929 design borrows from the Romanesque and Byzantine; it is, according to the venerable Institute of American Architects, the most phallic skyscraper in the history of architecture, thanks to its protruding glans, complete with slit. Today it is the chief domain of Brooklyn's orthodontists. To reach the viewing platform, you have to change elevators on the twenty-sixth floor. Height: end to end, five hundred and twelve feet.

At about the point where you'd start to slip on the condom is a clock. It tells Max he is slightly ahead of his own schedule. After checking his watch, he attempts a simple calculation involving the number of minutes left to complete two hours and the number of miles left to complete half of twenty-six-point-two. He has to restart the calculation several times. The brain resists — it knows it should be devoting its efforts to reconstructing, in three dimensions, a space occupied by tired, tired muscles.

The Academy of Music — 1908, neo-Renaissance — goes by, then the Fort Greene Historic District of Lafayette, its houses crowned by ancient (that is, mid-nineteenth century) Corinthian pediments. The oldest house is a farm, dating from 1812, wholly intact. The blue line goes right past it. A little further on is a Masonic temple whose façade bears reproductions of Greek motifs from the fifth century before Christ: the age of the battle of Marathon. The houses in this district are

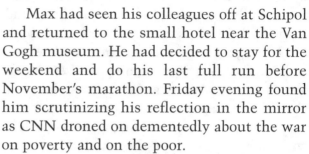

no higher than three stories, and the steps up to the front doors are as steep as those of Amsterdam...

* * *

Max had seen his colleagues off at Schipol and returned to the small hotel near the Van Gogh museum. He had decided to stay for the weekend and do his last full run before November's marathon. Friday evening found him scrutinizing his reflection in the mirror as CNN droned on dementedly about the war on poverty and on the poor.

His features are not worn or withered, but a few of the creases in his face are here to stay, notwithstanding the application of a costly lotion that concludes his daily shave. One furrow that runs vertically from the left-hand corner of his mouth appeared in the constellation less than a year ago. Also on the left, a raised spot — worryingly red — needs to be kept under surveillance, small though it is. His right eyelid droops slightly; the medical term is ptosis. Smile-lines are etched symmetrically from the nostrils down to the lower lip, and the razor cannot get in there to scythe off nascent whiskers without the help of the other hand to stretch the skin. His hair has apparently decided not to take leave of his head as quickly as he had feared when he was forty. Some graying has occurred, just enough to draw a line between himself and the young women he's stared at from the sidewalk cafés of Amsterdam. The social insignia are clear: short hair, classic silk tie, no longer tempted (given an architect's salary) into shoplifting.

Behind the mirror, Max (apparently) is what he is; he reminds himself only of himself. Glowing health: no sinister symptoms. Confident of the future, at least over the next few weeks. Sufficiently detached to visualize his running self. Not denying his past, but having coming to terms with it, like many of his generation who have finally put their lives in some kind of order. The rest are already dead, or alcoholic, or insane.

The infiltrator remains keenly alert to the world around him, ready to bite the hand of society as it feeds him, and flee.

Max can see what he has made of himself. He believes that once you are over forty you become responsible for the face you present to the world. He has, in consequence, chosen this body. It matches both his own demeanor and the role he has decided to play in society.

Had he been a generation younger he would have modeled himself on Jorge Semprun. A generation before that, Sartre (minus the lazy eye), and twenty years earlier, Malraux, but without the exaggeration. Further back, a surrealist with real social commitment — but not André Breton. Around the beginning of the century, it would have been Apollinaire and his war wounds, or Sir Arthur Conan Doyle. Ideal figures all, but Max does not claim to be their direct descendant. They are more like landmarks on a map: like the hairstyles teenagers choose out of a catalogue. That's what writers are good for.

Tomorrow he will go to Vondel Park. To run. Not to ponder, like Rousseau's solitary walker, nor the Parisian flâneur. Wandering the streets was enough for previous generations, enough for Baudelaire, whose giant's wings prevented him from flying. Max is hoping to steal a march on all of them — hoping he will get to run an extra lap or two in his life.

Whereas Giangiacomo was already dead at the age of forty-five. He had published Che Guevara's diary, *One Hundred Years of Solitude*, Reich and Pasternak. His millions had supported movements (Algerians, Sardinians, Cubans, in no particular order) while his entrepreneurial flair had covered Europe with the poster image of a Christlike face: Che lives!

The news came of his death, ripped to shreds on an electricity pylon in Segrate, outside Milan. One leg had been found twenty yards from his body, blown away by the fourth pack of dynamite (the other three had held fast). At first they believed it to be no accident but an act of provocation, since his face, buried in earth, had not been touched. And no one in the underground would carry a picture of his wife on him, or a fake ID with his true date of birth: June 19, 1926. But in the end they had to face facts. They gave him a hero's burial. He was their Victor Hugo, their Pierre Goldman — a revolutionary fallen in the class war, they said. He had opened their eyes, shown them the way. They daubed the walls of their communal kitchens with slogans that promised an early end to the oppression of the bosses and the bourgeoisie. They listened to the cassette he had recorded in his final hours, in which he admitted he was "not much good at manual work" but expressed confidence that his final gesture would help advance the cause of the public transport workers' strike by knocking out the power supply.

They — the immigrants, the students, the women — vowed to follow his example and rewire the whole continent with the red current of their anger.

Ingeborg's only camouflage is her name. It is the only one she will answer to. Those who can't get their tongues around its consonant clusters call her l'Allemande: the German woman. She speaks other languages with the same crisp, rather nasal staccato that characterizes her mother tongue, in which the letter O is often a feminine ending. Max eventually learned that her given name meant "green war" in Japanese. But it was never to be used, and Max had to promise as much before, one night, in a moment of weakness, she revealed it to him.

Yet that name suits her body to perfection, from her fringed, never serious eyes, to the jet black of her hair, as unvarying as the volcanic rock of Mount Unzen, right down to her forearms, her hairless legs, the rounded heels of her feet.

Max learned as a child that each race has a particular body odor. When black businessmen had come to stay at his parents' house he would sneak into the guest's room and see if any evidence — if no trace of color, then an identifiable smell — lingered on the sheets. The manager of a cement factory once affably let him in on the secret: white people smell of death, Orientals smell of damp laundry.

That was why, when Max kissed the German woman, his nostrils had flared in anticipation of his first ethnic embrace, but they had hardly drawn apart before she said: you're wearing Antheus by Chanel. All he had detected on her was another aromatic concoction sold throughout the world, but whose name he did not know.

That was long ago, in Europe, before he had emigrated to America. They were the pampered babies of the postwar boom, and they had loved each other to... distraction? Wasn't that the name of a perfume?

* * *

This was the fourth and last village before the pass and the city below. The ascent to the col was already palpable along its main street.

Where the road widened to make room for the main square (town hall, church and inn), he could almost smell where he had sat down to eat on a previous reconnaissance mission. Steak, fries and green beans. The thought made him hungry, but the last cooking odors from the inn had long since dispersed. He could detect no aroma of freshly baked bread, nor any sound from any house.

He could have taken a detour, describing the arc of a circle to reach the other end of the village, but the lie of the land was unsuitable. There was no point in expending such effort if it did not significantly improve his chances. He reached the furniture factory, at the southern end of the main street, without hindrance. He was virtually certain there had been no one: not a soul to remember him.

9
LAFAYETTE AVENUE

Taking a step was no longer, for me, simply taking a step, but rather, feeling where I was taking
my head. Is that something one can understand? Legs that obey, one after the other, and a
vertical posture over the ground that has to be
maintained. For my head, overflowing with
waves, unable to control its own whirlwinds —
my head feels all the whirlwinds from the earth
below that unbalance it and prevent it from
remaining upright.

Antonin Artaud, *Les Tarahumaras*

F urther down Lafayette Avenue, after the
historic houses in neat Dutch rows, come
massive apartment blocks that the city rents
to blacks who can guarantee an income. The
blue line then turns left onto Bedford Avenue,
past the fire station of the 34th Battalion,
home to Engine Company 209 and Ladder
Company 102. Apparently the New York Fire
Department's mission is not so much to fight
fires as to scare them off with bold displays of
hoses and helmets, shiny engines and ladders,
electronic control panels, gleaming nickel,
chrome, copper and brass.

Once again his gaze is fixed on a pair of
shoulders just ahead. This time it's an antinuclear T-shirt that has mesmerized him. A runner, fiftyish, like Max, who must be aiming for

the same time, or a bit faster — a useful pace setter. He glides by other shirts moving at a more leisurely pace, but always finds the nuclear power plant shaped like a death's head just a few strides in front of him. Now it seems to be slowing — no, it keeps going. Max decides to stay with his pacemaker, runs past busy knots of volunteers manning the tables on either side of the street, dodges dozens of paper cups splattered over the blue line.

Someone has become Max's personal trainer without knowing it, just as Max's blue with orange stripes may have become a beacon for someone else behind him. The world — inside this surging crowd — is thus reduced to one or two individuals: focal points unaware of their own significance. In such a world, even the most desperate have someone to latch on to. The last straggler will cross the finish line after midnight. In a unique dispensation for this kind of event, officials allow the race to go on as long as there's still a competitor willing to complete the course.

If you weren't following the blue line but continued up Lafayette, you would come upon Prospect Park, an excellent place for soft ground training. On one side of the park is the Brooklyn Museum, where Max has stood before the painting of Lake Geneva executed by Gustave Courbet during his exile in Switzerland. He had found refuge on its shores after reputedly blowing up the Vendôme Column during the Paris commune. It was from Max's home town of Ornans that he had fled, over the gentle slopes of the Jura, across the pine-studded plains, seeking the wedge of sky in the mountain ridge. Under the very nose of the police, he had reached the col, looked out over the plateau, and hurried down. He was granted a lifetime right of asylum.

He had sided with the Communards, destroyed a monolithic symbol of the ruling class, and fled. Call me Gustave...

Running is something physical, obviously. But seriously. Like Antonin Artaud's psychedelic experience among the Tarahumara, or like architecture. It's in the body, in the bone. Max's hand can keep drawing even when his brain is exhausted; the play of light on space and volume can make him lightheaded. He gets excited over a box of Rapidographs or a blue sketch pencil, loves the sound tracing paper makes when he tears it across the drawing board or the snap of a rubber band around a roll of photoengravings, smelling faintly of ammonia. A well-executed drawing fills him with admiration: he moves closer, removing his glasses, lets his eyes follow the shading, congratulates the draftsman. His heart truly rejoices at the sharply rendered detail in the depiction of two contiguous volumes. Everything marks him as a member of the brotherhood, from the trim cut of his clothes to the life of his mind, rooted in the physical world. Anxious to relax; hair kept short or tied at the back, whichever is in fashion. An irrational resistance to computer-assisted design. Loves construction sites — strolls around them even on weekends, discussing types of concrete with the foreman, studying the position of some formwork. Savoring the finer points: hollow joints, converging angles, bottlenose roundings. (But site meetings, surveying and dynamiting are left to others: not his department.)

As if on a protest march, Max has taken to the street, from where he can size up the cityscape which his fellow architects have left to posterity. Like an Amerindian on the warpath.

* * *

It was easy to obtain dynamite. A tunnel was under construction in the Jura foothills; all they needed was to do a bit of reconnaissance at one of the work sites and then, one mild summer evening, borrow a car from a colleague (one who was sympathetic, but not involved — in case they came to a police checkpoint). They didn't even have to break the door down; a crowbar in the lock did the trick. They loaded up the trunk with eleven boxes of Volumex, leaving the twelfth behind so that the proletariat could get on with its work. The lifting and carrying left their shoulders tense and sore all that night. Each box contained five packs of ten sticks. Each stick weighed two hundred grams.

Volumex is normally for pack explosions — in this instance, it would have been used to fill in the tunnel's temporary shafts. For them, what it lacked in quality was made up for in quantity.

They did not go back to town. At two in the morning, with lights still on here and there, it was hardly advisable to be moving around with concealed explosives. They dumped them near the spot where, later that day, they would be hidden according to the procedure outlined in *Le Petit Von Dach Illustré,* the training manual that every officer in the Swiss Army knew by heart (and whose publishers could never understand why it sold so well in "alternative" bookstores). Make a hole, 1.5 meters deep. Line with plastic garbage bags. Cover with a laundry basket placed upside down. Seal with sheets of tarpaper. They included a warning note, with an Italian translation, in case a child happened to discover it: DO NOT TOUCH! Alert the police or the pastor of your church. After the final scattering of dead leaves, they sprinkled black pepper all around to deter the gendarmes' sniffer dogs. Every so often one of them would make a discreet tour of inspection.

Then came the day they opened the cache and took out the amount required for the expedition, then carefully covered it over again. Surgical gloves ensured that they left as few traces as possible.

* * *

The third village lay on the final shelf before the ridge crest. He took a semicircular route through the cherry orchards so as not to disturb its inhabitants, who snored behind open shutters. Every twist and turn was known to him from the map. A double line two hundred meters before the first farm indicated a dirt track, where he turned right and continued until he came to the single thin line: a windbreak of poplar trees along a brook, which he crossed. Then he continued on his arc, winding around the cemetery. The moon had again disappeared behind the mountain ridge, but his dark shadow falling on patches of snow might be seen from any number of windows in the village. His pace quickened. He tried to land each time on the ball of his foot rather than the heel. The schoolhouse clock told him he had three quarters of an hour for the final climb, plus half an hour to cover any unforeseen delay.

The only sounds were his breathing, the muffled crunch of his footfalls, a slight rustle of wind in the branches. No sound of running water, though. It had frozen solid in the fountains and rivulets.

But why was there a light shining from the last farm in the settlement?

He could not avoid coming nearer. It might be a henhouse, a trick to promote egg-laying through the hours of darkness. He was only a Molotov cocktail's throw from the source of the light, and by now a gentle humming was audible: a generator, no doubt.

He had reached the far end of the vegetable garden, and was no further from the outbuilding than the length of a row of winter cabbage.

Suddenly the noise increased tenfold: the roar of a jumbo jet taking off. He froze in his tracks, a pillar of salt at the bottom of the garden. In a second the searchlights would pin him against the wall. Paralyzed, unable to make sense of the sound that assaulted his ears, he reached deep into his lungs, from which a plume of condensation emerged, and prepared his statement. I consider myself to be a political prisoner.

After a moment he could distinguish a medley of metallic noises from the stable, the sloshing of liquid, the lowing of cattle. He crept up to a high window, through which he could see siphons attached to udders and a farmer intent on the morning's quota of milk. Max took his courage in both feet and sprinted off towards the road that led out of the village.

10
LYNCH STREET

But I was almost running by now, and too out of breath to utter any such word. If only he would slow down a little, oh Marcus, just a tiny bit. If he would just reduce his rate of acceleration, well, it might be all right. But no, he ran, he was flying, so to speak, and there were moments — longer and longer moments, but at the same time they were, I don't know, shorter and shorter — because he was speeding up, he was actually increasing his acceleration rate, so there were times when neither of his feet was touching the ground.

Gilles Carpentier,
Hausmann m'empêche de dormir

Y ou empty your bladder right at the start. Women have portable cabins, while the men stand before a panoramic urinal.

It is not only through the pores that fluids are eliminated. The kidneys are sorely tested; every marathoner shows traces of blood in the urine by the end, due to microscopic lesions resulting from repetitive shock. There are more toilets at the tenth mile, but they're always full. And every minute counts. Which explains the spontaneous mass pit-stop at one of the vacant lots sandwiched between the burnt-out (you might think bombed-out) buildings along Bedford Avenue. There are not many spectators around. Men unhesitatingly drop their shorts; women squat without

embarrassment, legs barely apart. Those whose digestion has gone haywire from the exertion take this opportunity for relief as well, wiping themselves afterwards with handfuls of grass. It is all very comical, leading to a kind of congratulatory banter: That's better, isn't it! (If the first language doesn't seem to register, try another: *Ça soulage, n'est-ce pas?*)

Max lifts one side of his shorts, and while urinating slowly rolls his head in a circle from shoulder to shoulder, relaxing his neck, gazing at the few fast-moving clouds, white against an autumn sky more dazzling than the blue line. He doesn't really need to go, but might as well. One less thing. *Homo sapiens non urinat in ventum.*

Three Japanese men, not young, having pulled down their silk tights, are giggling and pointing at one another. Either some taboo has been breached, or there's a particularly vulgar side to Japanese culture. The three of them look so alike that they could run under one assumed name. Like the Korean in Berlin, in 1936, given an alias and forced to run for the Empire under the banner of the Rising Sun. The next time you see him, he's in the stands at the Barcelona Olympics, fifty-four years later, savoring sweet revenge when a young compatriot crosses the finish line, denying a son of his former colonizers the gold medal.

An alias, like Ingeborg: deception is sometimes necessary, if the cause is just. Max would love to have seen Jesse Owens thumb his nose at the Nazis, but all he knows of Berlin is the arrivals hall at Tempelhof, the desolate life of the junkies, and a certain nostalgia for the Wall, now that it's been pushed east.

For the time being he is heading for that twenty-mile Wall. And the only desolation he knows is the one that comes sometimes, around five in the afternoon, when he leaves the office. A quick mental calculation tells him that he has spent more time working for life as it is than against it, more time surviving than questioning. As an intellectual, he revels in the insertion of doubt between the established order of things and their prescribed destiny. It takes hold of him, at the wheel of his BMW, or just when he switches off the lamp over his drawing board. What have you done today? Time to get a gin tonic down your throat.

There are other days when things add up. Days when, as Ingeborg would say, you've scored a point against the lobby. You've snatched time away from necessity and given it to new possibilities: you've refused to approve a flawed underground garage scheme for a freight terminal, you didn't design a top-security prison or a "home" for the old to die in. You've agreed to see a student, soon to be an architect, and inspired him to seek utopia in his art, to resist enslavement to prevailing fashion. And managed not to blow your cover.

* * *

For years, they had this recurring nightmare. Where were you on the night of the explosion? Usually the setting is a basement of the federal police headquarters. Interrogators shine blinding lights in their eyes, smoke hangs in the air, the penal code lies on the table in front of them. But never would they spit it out, though they could feel the clammy prison at their backs. Never betray any emotion, never allow the adversary that handle on them. Concentrating on one thing, their cause. A just cause.

Awaking with a jolt, they would rehearse the increasingly unlikely scenario. The detec-

tive would say: We have evidence... I think this little conversation will interest you... And they'd play back a tape recording of the wife murmuring words of love to another, or making obviously coded remarks (Don't forget your gloves, it's cold out tonight). Or an unfamiliar voice, in accusing tones: Some people do their shopping at construction sites in the foothills of the Jura... They honed their psychological preparation for the ordeal to come. No cooperation. No pretense of surprise or concern. I don't intend to answer your questions, as I have nothing to say on the subject.

Questions that never came. The cops had lost the battle. No further action. The cast of a shoeprint gathered dust on a shelf; a badly typed report detailed their probable weight, sex, tendency to stoop, walking speed at the moment of imprint. The analysis of document fragments found at the scene revealed further clues. The "D" of DANGER! was probably written by a left-handed male. The policeman's approach to literary history.

And they would fall back asleep with still-warm memories, while the chief (federal) investigator summoned the team to his office for a final briefing, indicated the fifteen (federal) fileboxes, thanked everyone (in the name of the confederation) for their help and suggested they all adjourn for a drink at the Federal Café, just across the street. Dismissed!

* * *

He did not take the main road from one village to the next, but kept to an unpaved track that ran parallel to it and led to a campsite, whose chief attraction could not have been sunlight and warmth. Even the moon was unable to make an appearance here, between the two steep sides of the valley. This was terrain meant only for passing through. There was barely room for the two roads, a stream — now frozen into silence — and the railway line to the city of Olten, via a tunnel through the Jura. He knew that he would see flashes of blue light from the engine's pantograph in the unlikely event the train was running ahead of schedule; but the commuters were still sound asleep.

The cliff beyond the campsite loomed menacingly, so dark it was nearly invisible. He concentrated on the frozen puddles in the road. Soon he came to a kind of trailer cemetery: mobile homes mounted on blocks, occupied a few weeks in the year.

Sure he would encounter no living soul, he found he was enjoying this shortcut. Registering only the sound of his own steps, he crossed a line of antitank defenses that ran perpendicular to the valley: the usual boxlike concrete structures, not marked on the map. Casting an almost benevolent eye over them, he detected the babble of rushing water beside a thicket of hazel trees. A cascade whose irregular flow kept it from freezing over.

He snapped off an icicle and sucked on it contentedly, feeling a renewal of energy. Ready to up the tempo. Who says crime doesn't pay?

11
BEDFORD AVENUE

Then, when he had run for a long time within the labyrinth, when he had passed through its thousands of rooms and corridors, when he had become utterly lost in all its twists and turns, in all its corners and recesses, in all its meandering bends with their doors, not always the same, and their walls, always the same, there came a moment when Icarus, exhausted, drained of all strength and heart, realized that there was no way out, not anywhere, that all his running was pointless and insane, that all his efforts were to no avail and all hope an illusion. So he stopped. And I can almost hear the sound of his breathing, and the silence within him like a death.

André Comte-Sponville,
Traité du désespoir et de la béatitude

As the blue line advances and the social economy declines, the number of unaccompanied children increases. Their principal amusement is to stretch out an open hand towards a runner at full stretch, offering to make contact. It is their bid for recognition: a struggling marathoner, they imagine, will remember how some kid on the sidelines that Sunday morning gave him a boost of strength. Sometimes they hold out a candy, unwrapped and already sticky, or a slice of tropical fruit. Take it! It'll help you win! There are small Asian girls with long hair, shaven-headed rappers, dark-eyed Latinos. Max is happy to give them the high-five. By tomorrow he won't be anyone's champion.

A little girl in a cheerless black dress, her face already framed by a headscarf, stands at a corner. She seems alone. No one accepts her offer of a palm to slap, for at this point the blue line veers off at an angle away from her. Max leaves the pack of runners he's with and heads towards her. Her face lights up as he approaches.

Just when his hand is about to touch hers, someone grabs her from behind and roughly yanks her back, yelling in a language that (to American ears) sounds German. Her father is dressed entirely in black.

Driven out of Hungary and Poland during World War Two, the Hassidic community settled along Bedford Avenue. Even before the war, Williamsburg was a neighborhood Orthodox Jews felt comfortable in. As their numbers increased they moved into other parts of Brooklyn. At 491 Bedford Avenue, in front of the synagogue, they stand with their backs to the semi-naked stream of runners — a sight that must be offensive to them. It reminds Max of the Paris-to-Dakar motor rally, its engine-roar shattering the tranquillity of an oasis of bemused locals. The Orthodox women, scarved and bewigged, are in long skirts; the bearded men, ringlets looped over their ears, wear black hats and coattails. Across the street, a plaque at 500 Bedford Avenue commemorates the house of Josef Teitelbaum, the great rabbi who organized the migration of Eastern European Jews.

The blue line continues under a railway bridge, its metal painted blue to match the blue of the nearby Williamsburg Bridge; and the sky is blue, all the way to the East Village, across the blue-splashed river, where the Big Apple is as blue as an orange.

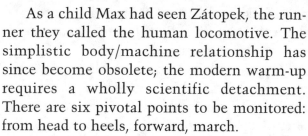

As a child Max had seen Zátopek, the runner they called the human locomotive. The simplistic body/machine relationship has since become obsolete; the modern warm-up requires a wholly scientific detachment. There are six pivotal points to be monitored: from head to heels, forward, march.

First, the neck. Rotate the head around the trunk, as if rolling on a ball bearing built into the spinal column.

Second, the shoulders. Raise them, break them down.

Third, the upper torso. Hands on buttocks, pivoting constantly.

Fourth, the hips. Twisting to the left, look back at your right heel. Twisting right, look back at your left heel.

Fifth, the knees. When you straighten up, you should not hear the crackle of grit around the kneecaps.

Sixth, the ankles. Rotate each foot in one direction, then the other.

Deep breaths now before stretching legs and arms. Leaning face forwards on a tree trunk, extend the back. Look up through the branches. Legs spread, hands clasped behind the back, bend forwards and raise the arms. Hear my prayer. Help me over the Wall.

Max has made a Historic Compromise with his body. His running style (it cannot be said too often) is based on a line-by-line study of the instructions set out in the book.

The chest is out, as if you were exhibiting your nipples. Hips, too, are thrust forward, as if you were exhibiting your genitals. This posture feels contrived at first, but hours of running confirm its efficacy. It allows you to maintain a near-vertical axis, so that the resulting forces go straight down to the ground. Unlike the oblique lines of fatigue he is running past just now.

The arms and legs, coupled in equal opposite movements, drive the vertical force forward, but Max's head runs on autopilot. Detached from the body's rhythmic tensions, it remains outside the system.

The legs must perform short, even strides, low over the ground, but mainly: always moving forward. An ideal already beyond the reach of an exhausted blond youth ahead, who's starting to waddle like a duck.

Meanwhile, the arms provide a countervailing swing. White-gloved palms turned downwards, staying as close as possible to Max's blue shorts.

* * *

They learned to slip surgical gloves quickly over their hands. Dusted with talc, they formed a watertight envelope around perspiring fingers, like condoms. The alternative, small bandages taped over the fingertips so beloved of forensics, was particularly useful in situations where they had to move in public but incognito (posting a list of demands, for example), and leave no traces.

The Zurich police laboratory was the first in Europe to use electron microscopes, gas chromatography, suction devices for collecting microparticles from the body and clothing of fugitives. It had acquired an international reputation — quite apart from its graphology lab or its linguistic analysis unit, its specialists in applied anthropometry and its M.O. classification system — for its skill in retrieving evidence from clothing: a trace of pollen here (the suspect walked under a chestnut tree), a microfiber there (the suspect embraced the woman under the chestnut tree).

They studied these techniques in the libraries of the Federal Institute of

Technology, which readily issued them with readers' cards. And they took precautions others might think bordered on paranoia: a complete change of clothes after every operation, burning their gloves after one use (because fingerprints would be deposited on the inside surface), always wearing a cap or wig so as not to leave a single hair behind, showering with the thoroughness of someone who has just been exposed to radiation, never going to the toilet along the way, reversing the tires of a bicycle used on a dirt track. It was an approach that, with constant practice, became second nature.

They were quietly amused to read in the Journal of Police Forensics (also available in the libraries) that the saboteurs had, regrettably, devised increasingly sophisticated means of eluding detection. It is therefore inevitable, according to one, that the taxpayer will have to pay more if this first-rate public service is to keep pace with developments.

* * *

Without even raising his eyes above the jagged line of treetops, Max could see the almost horizontal stripe of a vapor trail, ghostly blue in the moonlight. At this time of night only a few intercontinental airports were still open, so it would be a transatlantic flight landing in Milan at six, or possibly at Rome a few minutes later. Breakfast was no doubt being served as the descent from twelve thousand feet commenced. The temperature up there would now be rising, after the minus fifty Centigrade of the lower stratosphere. Higher yet, a slow-moving star. The satellite was recording the planet's every suspicious movement — the advancing zone of sunlight, a stationary high over the Azores, a smog cloud over the Maldives, lunchtime traffic in Tokyo, a column of smoke from a campfire on Everest. The satellite did not, however, capture the plume of vapor expelled with a gasp by a solitary runner on the dark side of the planet.

12
MANHATTAN AVENUE, BROOKLYN

> The cold air should have, the cold air clang-
> ing and banging in my head while I'm running
> down the sidewalk, the cold air could have
> stopped me [...]
> I've been running too long, I can't go on. I
> have two little wings at the top of my back that
> let me float above the sidewalk, and he is not
> far away now, and there he is in the Museum
> gardens, thinking he can get away from me!
>
> Anne-Lise Grobéry, *Infiniment plus*

The blue line comes to Greenpoint, where the clapboard houses are only two stories high. You half expect to see the sheriff appear on a rooftop, ready to draw, while the bad guy (hidden, but in full view of the camera) lines up the sights on his rifle. But the saloon is closed and the hitching-post is a parking meter. Across the river, the famous beveled silhouette of the Citicorp Building glints with the saber-strike of the sun gods.

A little further on is a mock-up of a Chicago street from the Thirties. Gangsters are captured here — by film crews — as they speed out of town in a hail of bullets; nearby, there are warehouses full of brand-new, burnt-out cars. The Western endures, in spirit. This is where, around 1860, ships were being built for the whole wide world.

The area is currently in transition. Its location on the East River is too desirable to be left to warehouses but not yet desirable enough for luxury condos overlooking Manhattan at sunset. But for the pounding of running feet, the sharp rise of property values along this stretch would be audible.

In 1859, Charles Pratt, the streetlighting magnate, inaugurated the first kerosene refinery here. Just beyond it, he built the Astral Apartments, where his workers dreamt their dreams. They're already being redeveloped and renovated.

At the corner of Manhattan and Milton, the spire of St. Anthony of Padua climbs to two hundred and forty feet while the blue line takes another bend and heads off towards the copper onion domes of the Cathedral of the Transfiguration. Louis Allmendiger's 1921 design, based on the Winter Palace in St. Petersburg, coincided with the arrival of numerous Russian Orthodox émigrés. They are congregated before it now, the service over, and great square beards cheer the runners on.

At each new corner he looks down the street to Manhattan. Many people in this part of Brooklyn will never even set foot there, where Max lives.

Slim, graying hair, very slightly stooped owing to his height, untinted glasses, suitable necktie. Outside the office, he wears a black Chevignon leather jacket, Levi's 501s, white Reeboks, a silk shirt with front pockets for his pencil and sketchbook. He sketches wherever, whenever. On his travels. At sidewalk cafés. A piece of frontage, a detail on a balustrade. Axonometric projections for a new structure awaiting its shell. He keeps up with his peers, reads the publications, enters the competitions, discusses the latest projects. It always makes him smile when they say they've "just built

something", given that construction workers are the only ones who can say so truthfully. Architects work on representations of things — a crucial business nonetheless, to judge by Max's passion for it. For he will stop anywhere, close one eye, check an alignment, stretch out an arm, calculate a ratio or the length of a plumb line. He does not sketch trees, other than the neatly pruned prototypes he might incorporate into a drystone design feature. He is not an artist, but you cannot take the art out of architecture. Instead, Max is trying to be a master craftsman within his profession, wise in the ways of the businessman and the promoter, versed in the skills of the technician and the engineer, designing the esthetics of his own life: his own work of art. Why look for something else? He can be many men in this trade: like the great lover who, in one woman, knows all the women he will never embrace.

The calling is in his blood; it is his life's blood. In all seasons, with never a regret. How can one be anything other than an architect? Skeleton and skin, light and shade, microcosm and macrocosm. Even God chose to be an architect. The evil of computers is that their architecture is not open enough. Mies Van der Rohe said architecture was his mistress, and Le Corbusier told his new wife: My life as an architect will be a hard one, and you will have no children.

Construction, deconstruction: on the satanic side of the profession, you learn how to position an explosive charge to bring down a building or rip out a wall. As part of his training in basic civil engineering, Max went on a course. He quickly acquired the knack. How to make a factory chimney collapse neatly to one side with a single sandbag and three kilos of dynamite; how to section an H beam with the precise placement of a few sticks of

blasting gelatin. Power pylons pose an especially fascinating problem in statics when torsion comes into play, the moment three of the
four potential sections are no longer equidis-
tant from the ground.

But now, technology is draining all the
blood from the profession. Every airport under
construction looks like every other airport
under construction. Air cargo terminals are
full of containers; the containers are full of
parts for building new air cargo terminals.

Max tries his answering machine, but the line
is busy. Tries again. This time Ingeborg is there.

"I saw your name on the list, Max." The
voice in his headband is buoyant. "Are you
trying to lose weight?"

This might get him going: it's the one thing
he has never worried about. Max, who will be
skinny from cradle to grave, can give ten good
reasons for his running, but not that one.

"Don't play games. Where are you?"

Where indeed? The German woman is an
ethereal being, located somewhere that is
always nowhere. No time zone can contain
her; she has no continental or sentimental
ties. An eternal traveler among the satellite
links. And when you go to hold her, you find
she is already taken.

Max pictures a wicker armchair on a terrace overlooking Nagasaki Bay.

Three years ago, she had left her number
on his answering machine. When his work
took him to Nagasaki, where they had been
together sixteen years earlier, he phoned her
from his hotel. They talked at length about
what each was doing or about to do in that
month of July, and agreed to meet the next
day. She sounded energetic, positive. She
spoke repeatedly of the past, their past.

Her current job was something to do with
the European export market of a top Japanese

fashion designer. She invited him to join her in Paris, or Amsterdam.

She still believed in direct action: never give the lobby breathing space.

I'll call you tomorrow, Max. We'll meet up. But she didn't, and he awoke, sobbing, from his dreams, with the realization that she could love only at a distance. Had she grown obese, become ugly, got married...?

"What stage are you at now, Max?" In his headband now, her mouth very close to the microphone. Out of doors, judging by the background noise.

"Twelfth mile. Manhattan Avenue, in Brooklyn."

"You're doing six miles an hour then. You should finish in under four hours. Is that what you're aiming for?"

"Yes." He's beginning to feel winded. "Could we talk some other time? I've got so much to ask you."

"Really? About Nagasaki?"

Max brings his wristband to his lips, about to answer, but she has hung up on him. She does not wish to talk about their past, about Nagasaki, a long time ago.

It was July. This was her city, but they had gone to a hotel and checked into an air-conditioned room. The view from the window was of Nagasaki Bay and the Mitsubishi shipyards, the biggest dry dock on the planet. Two kilometers up the valley is the hypocenter, as the Japanese call the point of maximum heat and radiation from the American bomb. Several members of Ingeborg's family developed cancer; she herself was born two months after the blast. Pediatricians fitted her with a brace, because they thought her hipbones would atrophy. They were wrong.

A hotel room where they left their shoes outside, next to the plastic ones for use in the bathroom. On the tatami, two mattresses side by side, two bowls of green tea, a lit cigarette. The waning light of evening. He got lost in her hair; she whispered Hold me tighter. He scratched his skin on her earrings.

One of life's coincidences finds Max once more in this martyred city, alone. He is there to help inaugurate work on the air cargo terminal at Nagasaki's international airport. He strolls down to the harborfront; the hotel is still there. Other couples now squeeze each other tighter. The German woman is somewhere very near, but she will not see him. She may have gone on one of her undercover eco-missions, or joined a worldwide conspiracy, or been arrested by the lobby. Perhaps she has a jealous husband. The telephone makes deception easy.

Today Max will not ask her about Nagasaki, except to say that he'll be going back there soon for the job assignment phase of the operation, so why not take this opportunity to — ? No, neither of them has any taste for emotional leftovers.

But he doesn't understand the reason for these two calls from her. Why now, in the midst of this test he has set himself? To cheer him on, or up? Give him her support, at long last? Give him something to run for — some promise of a reward?

A simple phone call is anything but simple as far as Max is concerned. He had so often hoped she would call him, just to re-establish the meeting of minds. When he first came to New York (before he lived on 90th Street, among the yuppies) he would check his incoming messages in the hope that, just once...

But no. Her motto: if your phone doesn't ring, it's me.

* * *

He made ready to vote with his feet and a few sticks of dynamite.

He observed the night watchman's routine, noted the pattern of traffic on local roads after midnight, checked the schedule of overnight freight trains. He measured every angle of the condemned structure, the profile and section of its metal pillars. Each calculation, once committed to paper, was carefully concealed among the children's drawings in the communal playroom.

It took an hour to drive from his workplace to the theater of operations. He parked at a housing estate nearby; his car, with its local licence plates, went unnoticed, and the good citizen (out walking his dog after the late news and before the final turn of the lock) saw nothing to remark in the jogger who trotted by. He seemed no different from the other commuters, who did not socialize in any case, unless their dogs were the same breed or their children went to the same school. The chemical industry might describe itself as one big family, but its workers pretended not to belong to it the minute they got home; in fact, that was how they could be recognized.

The condemned structure was nearly a mile from any dwelling. At the appointed hour on the appointed day, there would be no risk to life, only to sleep.

As he drove home from each reconnaissance mission, he recorded all his observations on a dictaphone. Later he would transcribe them, work them into his calculations, memorize the conclusions, then wipe the tape and burn the paper. He had to assume that the knock at the door, if it came at some ungodly hour in the morning, would not (nowadays, anyway) be the milkman.

When the day came, he was there, in the early evening, by the exhibition hall.

The material was ready: temporary detour signs to ward off any traffic, as well as a big placard that would scare off the night watchman, should he be tempted to investigate further: DANGER! RISK OF EXPLOSION — Prohibited Area — Alert the police. Plus all the supplies needed for the mission, including a change of clothes, any trace of which at the crime scene could be used as evidence and must therefore be destroyed.

★ ★ ★

There was no need for a flashlight. The moon was just bright enough to show him the way up to the second village without casting a silhouette. He could make good time here. Some distance before the crossroads, he struck off to his left, detouring onto hard snow — thus avoiding the farm whose buildings occupied all four corners of the intersection, and whose dog, whether or not it was chained up, would be sure to take notice of the passing stranger.

He could hear the nation's flag flapping in the west wind.

The approach to the village was lined with wealthy homes, nearly all with two-car garages (or at least carports) and at least two Mercedes per family. He adopted the gait of the late-night reveler in need of another drink before facing the wife — or so it would appear to any insomniac who happened to glimpse him from the bathroom window. The map was under his jacket, his gloves were right for the season, his scarf concealed the lower part of his face and his hat the top.

He came to the hotel. Someone was playing a fife; other partygoers slumped at the table in an alcoholic doze. The carnival, with its pipes and drums, had not stopped for a week since Ash Wednesday. The one hundred and

fifty meters from one end of the hotel to the other were more perilous to him than the many miles of open country. Almost keeping time with the plaintive little melody as he strolled by — off to the bakery to get the first croissants of the day? — he soon came to the last house in the village. Without hindrance.

A yellow sign pointed to the third village, forty-five minutes away. He would take another route, parallel to the main road, and do it in barely half the time. Expelling one deep breath in a billow of smoke, he was off again. A fugitive, gently on the run.

13

PULASKI BRIDGE

This one was a still youngish man, in a blue
tracksuit and white running shoes, coming out
of the alley just to the left of Michel's Bench. He
sped past him the first time, snorting like a seal.
He did a complete lap of the Roundabout, on
the tree-lined side. Michel watched the Jogger
closely until the instant he passed in front of
him a second time, noticeably wearier and with
big beads of sweat pouring off him. His wheezing, fitful run then proceeded in a second,
smaller circle: around the Pool. With his fixed
stare — for, despite his fatigue, he kept his head
resolutely upright — the Jogger trotted and
turned as though he could see nothing and no
one. Not the sky, nor the trees, nor the Pool nor
the Swan nor the Crazy Old Man, and of course
not Michel, whom he ran past a third and final
time, panting, his face streaming, before taking
off down the first alley to the right of the Bench.

Nicolas Morel, *Double Aveugle*

T he marathon's halfway point is situated
on Pulaski Bridge, which takes you out
of Brooklyn into Queens. Polish diplomats
see to it that once a year the national colors
are hoisted here in honor of Casimir Pulaski,
a young cavalry officer killed while leading
the attack on Savannah in 1779. Almost from
the day it was completed in 1954, this span
over Newton Creek has been under repair or
renovation, and only one lane is open. This,
coupled with the slowing effect of the gradi-
ent, causes a bottleneck to form. It is an

opportunity for those runners with less than two hours of active service in their legs to hail one another and trade congratulations on reaching the point where the blue line is shorter ahead than behind. They all hope to finish in four hours.

On the left, midtown Manhattan stands out sharply against an immaculate autumn sky. The most endearing silhouette belongs to the Chrysler Building, not just for its scrolled arcs throwing floodlit reflections on cigarette billboards, but for its automorphism, if that is the term: from the ground, its crown mimics a radiator grille. Its cathedralesque gargoyles, at control-tower height, are pinned above Max's drawing board:

Further up the river, a column of ants — whose leaders will be crossing the finish line in just ten minutes — leaves Queens and passes through the metal grid of the Queensboro Bridge to enter Manhattan. A shaven-headed Mexican named Garcia heads the men's field. His image inspires little affection. Compare Bikila, who ran barefoot, with this career soldier who raises Dobermans and gives them names like Hitler, Qaddafi and Che Guevara. He never removes his white gloves, not even to wave to the crowd applauding his triumph.

The bridge slopes gently downhill now, an opportunity to exercise different sets of muscles.

* * *

They openly despised sports, rejected the cult of the body, scorned the obsession with performance, loathed the system whereby champions were designated on the basis of points accumulated or time taken to complete a task, as on the assembly line. Football clubs were mere tools in the hands of the bosses, each promoting some local specialty: the automobile in Turin, banks in Zurich, property development in Frankfurt.

Only one exception to this line was admitted: boxing. The ring had enabled a few young blacks to reappropriate the wealth which corporate exploitation of their blues had robbed them of, and thus to score a point for the working classes. Their hatred for the athletic disciplines (discipline being the operative word) shielded them from ridicule. They couldn't kick a ball, or keep their balance; carrying an armful of political pamphlets left them gasping for breath. They all smoked, preferably strong Gauloises, like Giangiacomo, or the occasional cigar, a symbol shared by South American revolutionaries, capitalist bosses and Mafia dons in white spats. The only permissible physical exercise was swimming (for medical reasons) or downhill skiing, a local tradition which those born and bred in the mountains could not bring themselves to give up, despite the fact that it could not be ideologically justified.

They did not belong to the Californian tendency, with its non-violent Flower Power and quest for Eastern spirituality. When they went to Berkeley in 1971, they found barricades on Telegraph Avenue, boarded-up storefronts and the National Guard, shooting on sight. The rest — the gray heron's flight over the campus lake, joggers among the sequoias, skimpily clad students, Breasts Must Be Covered On University Premises — did not impress them. Berkeley was to be seen through the eyes of the Black Panthers, holed up a few miles away in Oakland, in the ghetto, or of Angela Davis, waving a gun at the judge, or of James Baldwin and *The Fire Next Time*.

They returned to the factory gates of Europe, convinced that the proletarian masses would soon turn their fire on the bosses.

Nascent feminists were informed that the only body that counts is the social body.

* * *

He was on the high plateau, the final shelf formed by the Jura before the ridge crest. This was family-Sunday-stroll territory: a straight, slightly downhill stretch where Daddy might let go of the buggy to the delight of Baby and the horror of Mom.

He upped the tempo a bit, though he was already a few minutes ahead of his schedule. A stand of mature walnut trees stood out against the moon's half-light, pockets of snow glinting in the rough bark. Slender cherry saplings were being prepared for their future contribution to the renowned local schnapps. Each was tied at the top to a thin wooden pole. The line of trees punctuated the route as far as the eye could see, disappearing in the night-blue contours of the slope ahead. The loveliness of the landscape forbade melancholy; leaving everything behind, he set his uncertain star on the great gash in the ridge ahead, its virgin snow glowing back at the moon.

Crisp footfalls on hard snow.

He fairly flew, as all the beauty of the world held its breath.

14
VERNON BOULEVARD

Selvy got a ride from a man in a pickup,
south from Marathon. The man was about sev-
enty-five years old. There was a deer rifle on a
rack at the back of the cab. Four hours till
nightfall. The desert. [...]
  A buzzard on a fencepost. Single windmill in
the distance. Everything here was in the distance. Distance was the salient fact. Even after
you reached something, you were immersed in
distance. It didn't end until the mountains and
he wasn't going that far.

Don DeLillo, *Running Dog*

The full weight of the Citicorp Building
(Skidmore, Owings and Merrill, 1989)
bears down on the blue line as it passes under
its forty-eight stories — the tallest skyscraper
outside Manhattan. Like the Williamsburg
Savings Bank in Brooklyn, it stands out for
miles around, a lone beacon. It is not so much
a phallus as a space shuttle poised for lift-off,
complete with vertical launching gantry in
tinted glass.

The other reference point for the people
of Queens is the tunnel to Manhattan,
financed in the last century by an industrial-
ist of genius with a modest sideline in piano-
building. Steinway himself lived further
north, but from the blue line you can see the

housing he provided for his workers: one of the many phalansteries built by nineteenth-century capitalists.

At 49th Street, a flag directs the blue line to the left. It takes Vernon Street as far as 44th, angles left onto Hunter Street and then turns twice again to the left, onto the ramp of the Queensboro Bridge. Thus concludes today's tour of the borough named for Charles II's queen, Catherine of Braganza. Home to two million people and two of New York's airports, whose activity Max follows from his office window: flashes of silver slipping below the horizon, a welcome distraction from the company of his colleagues.

Around noon he takes the elevator down to earth level. A few steps in the direction of the East Village to an eatery whose name consists of two numbers, one for the street and one for the avenue. Formica and imitation wood, no tablecloths, thirty or so customers, Turkish and Balkan men mainly. Only a couple of women, other than the one who runs the place. Its smoke lingers on his clothes for the rest of the afternoon. Food for thought, not the repetitive orthodoxy of the company cafeteria. With meetings all morning and more scheduled for the afternoon, Max's social calendar is as full as he wants it to be.

Smoking was hard to give up, but the craving is gone. Weekends are the worst. It is not the taste he misses but the social ritual, the sensuality of it, the nostalgia most of all: the German woman pulling the sheets up over her bare breast.

During the week, his colleagues provide plenty of other frustrations. He detests none in particular, but has only contempt for their unwavering corporate smugness, the way they inflate their "mission" with a significance it does not possess. In his attempts to puncture

their pretensions, it has become apparent that Max's style of conflict resolution is inappropriate. Problems, for them, are things to be numbered, or sequenced, but more importantly to be nurtured, so that they grow into matters of great weight, becoming in the end their own inviolable fiefdoms. Max looks at water flowing down a river: it goes around the rock. No one tries to compress it or stress it, or expects stone to dissolve on contact with it. When you step into it, the river always finds its way around your feet and back to the sea. With respect to Japanese philosophy, Max can draw on more than one metaphor as he sketches his thoughts. He dreams of solving everything the way you take on a marathon: impossible, until you have tamed it.

No less fascinating are the problems overheard in a bar in Tokyo: one man is complaining about his poor health, another stumbles out to get something to eat, but not at home, no way! At the next table, Arabic is being spoken, but Max picks out meal tickets, subway tokens, public showers in English, as he would catch yes or thank you in a local bar in another Japanese city, somewhere he might conceal the anonymity of his international executive persona.

Outside, the steam curls up from a grate, a cab goes by — yellow in New York, green in Nagasaki — and a vagabond with wild eyes stares at an empty display window, pulling his hood over his head. The bosses at world headquarters make you promise never to end up like that, always to have enough credit to pay within two months. Max adjusts his collar, pays cash, leaves a good tip and returns to the other world, the one his co-workers inhabit. The boundaries between the two worlds are blurred, and Max enjoys playing at the edges. But he has no wish to fall into the quicksand of chronic insecurity.

* * *

They lived communally, but whether out of duty, choice or economic necessity was not clear, unlike the theory behind it: the family, one of the unholy trinity alongside work and the fatherland, had to be done away with as quickly as possible to make way for the extended tribe, the communal household. The police knew the theory, too, and put the communes and their inhabitants on file.

They had always lived with others, but pursued their love affairs outside and usually slept alone, in double beds. The height of indulgence was to spend the morning in bed with their books or diaries. The stereos, bicycles and cars they possessed belonged to everyone and to no one, and they waged permanent war on the manifold aspects of individual property — seen not as an evil in itself, but as the fundamental blueprint for a social order that (were it to be perpetuated) would keep the immigrants in their slums, the homeless in their cardboard boxes, the blacks in their ghettos and the wives of the wealthy on the analyst's couch.

* * *

A flat road through beech and fir led to an isolated farm, marking the start of this final Jurassic shelf, and the end of his first survey map. He stopped, burnt it and covered the ashes with rocks, then unfolded the next in the series. Emerging from the woods, he expected to see a farm, but could hardly make it out at first. It lay further down and deeper in the ground than the map had seemed to indicate. He took another detour, so his scent would not wake the dogs or other farm animals. The odor on the snow-covered fields was that of the liquid manure farmers spread on their fields: come the thaw, it would penetrate all the more deeply into the earth. Nothing moved inside the four massive walls, hunkered down in the dark, sheltering from the winds off the mountain ridge. The moon would rise in a few minutes; he feared for his invisibility, but there was no one at the roadside to record his deeds.

Small outcroppings of dark earth, which hastened the melting of the thin crust of snow, showed the hound where to track down the mole, dazzled by daylight. But at this hour, all cats — or so it's said — are gray.

15

QUEENSBORO BRIDGE

> But now we had to hurry; the bus was waiting on the other side of the avenue. We were running across it. I was last. A car was coming but I had plenty of time. I ran but my damned ankle gave way right in the middle of the avenue and I went flying.
>
> I can still hear the screech of brakes, feel a tremendous crunch... then darkness...
>
> I woke up in the hospital three days later.
>
> Guy Lagorce, *Rue des Victoires*

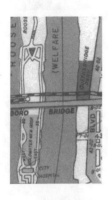

I n one of its recent wars, America bombed the enemy capital's bridges. According to the *New York Times*, "They are no different from us now — their bridges, too, are out of commission." It hasn't collapsed yet, but the Queensboro Bridge is in constant need of repair, for which the public purse provides scant funding. One lane or another is usually closed to traffic, while girders have to be patched and repainted, old welds strengthened and cladding replaced. As the blue line climbs onto the lower deck approach, it crosses the fifteen-mile mark; by the time it reaches the other side, sixteen miles have gone by. In between, it passes through a latticework of metal, beneath which the waters of the East River are visible, except where synthetic carpeting covers the expansion joints. At one hundred and fifty feet, this is the second highest point on the course, after the Verrazano-Narrows Bridge.

The Queensboro Bridge straddles the two arms of the river in a single arc, spanning the whole of Roosevelt Island. It was built in 1909, the same year as the Manhattan Bridge, and is held up by girders rather than cables. None of its three spans is the same; the great beams mesh impressively at the upper ends of the middle section. It is like running inside a cage. Through its steel bars, the eye of an architect can pick out the crème de la crème of Manhattan: Le Corbusier and Niemeyer's UN headquarters, parallel to the river, the starting point of yesterday's Breakfast Run; Mies Van der Rohe's Seagram Building at Park and 53rd, not far from the very grate that blew the steam up Marilyn Monroe's skirt; the truncated ellipsoid that Gropius placed across the geometry of the river; Johnson's two creations, one a lipstick, the other a post-modern Chippendale chest of drawers. And of course there is Max's cherished Chrysler Building, and the Empire State, and the Citicorp.

When Gatsby drives the narrator to Manhattan in his convertible, F. Scott Fitzgerald writes that the city seen from the Queensboro Bridge is always the city seen for the first time, in its first wild promise of all the mystery and the beauty in the world.

Max, that Saturday afternoon, had crossed the East River to train in accordance with his motto: run for sure, but take risks. On the return leg he took the Queensboro Bridge. Halfway across, the citybound lane had ground to a halt, and no traffic was coming through in the opposite direction. Then there were ambulances, police cars and television vans. A man was virtually hanging off the edge of the bridge, threatening to jump. One

cop crouched just three yards from him; the others hung back at a distance of ten yards. No one had thought to close the pedestrian lane, so that Max suddenly found himself trotting right into the middle of the scene. He froze, almost touching despair; behind him, a posse of hand-held cameras hoping to capture a moment of drama. Dead silence. High noon. Who would draw first? The cop nearest the man held a lasso. Not moving a muscle; he actually looked bored. A driver honked his horn. The man was about Max's age. He shifted, kneeling forward, stretching his arms. It looked as if he might be about to let go from exhaustion. He would have to talk to him ever so gently — tell him that Daisy was waiting, without Gatsby, at the Plaza. But if he jumped after all, Max would have it on his conscience. He decided to put his trust in the division of labor and admit that the cops might deal with the psychology of the situation better than he could. He averted his eyes when the suicidal gaze turned to him, and ran off.

At the other end of the bridge a policeman asked him if they'd gotten the guy, and whether it would be over soon. I couldn't watch, said Max. Someone said there had been another one, yesterday, on the Brooklyn Bridge.

Since that day Max had ceased to be an immigrant. It was his ceremony of initiation into the cowardice that makes life here possible.

Or rather, the indifference. Which he had learnt, the hard way, from the German woman's absences. How do you learn to forget? By living from day to day, the same way you get through withdrawal from nicotine or cocaine. The main thing is to give up. A pure, positively negative act. You set a course and follow it, looking the landscape square in the eyes: plant yourself before a tree and swear to it that you will free yourself from this dependence. Exercise the option to empty your mind, though thoughts may flood in without warning. Expect certain tell-tale signs that you will dismiss the moment they appear.

Max knows that there must be a chance they will one day be reunited, for the German woman is (unlike all others) the presence behind every crack in his universe.

The urge to smoke disappears as long as he's running, breathing deep. But it can always be reawakened by a chance encounter — a Japanese woman reading on a park bench, slender fingers toying with a cigarette lighter. Or a string of dogs chasing each other around a bed of tulips. Especially because of the tulips, her tulips, which stab at his heart and cloud his memory.

Waking up is harder than going to sleep, in Max's opinion, because it comes whenever it wants, leaving all his nightmares unresolved.

A beep in his headband. As he had anticipated: the German woman. For the third time, her message traverses the electromagnetic fields of the city to reach him.

"Where are you now, Max?"

"The western exit from Queensboro Bridge." An ant reporting its position on the planet to an interstellar control tower.

"So you'll finish in four hours. I'm going to finish less than an hour from now," said the voice in his headband.

"Finish what?" Max speaks into the microphone on his wrist without losing his rhythm.

"The New York City Marathon, in under three hours," said the voice, sounding genuinely winded.

"I know you can be in two places at once, Ingeborg, but a few minutes ago, you were –"

She's gone. End of conversation, or break in transmission? Max hates this teasing; it's a betrayal of the respect they owe one another, of the debt they contracted when they came together.

The most difficult part of the race is coming up now. His legs are growing stiff, and his stomach emits a strange gurgling sound. Not yet the twenty-mile Wall. As for your jokes, dear lady, we could do without them. And what if (Max hypothesizes) she were planning to meet him at the finish line — wouldn't that be just like her? A bouquet of tulips she would throw from the grandstand in Central Park, perhaps, or a walk through autumn leaves and a bowl of sake.

With the women he admires Max, the loner, can only have the most impossible relations. With the French woman, it's a power struggle, always falling out and making up; with the Italian, she's already halfway to the airport by the time Max is ready to join battle. As for the German woman, it's all distance, physical separation, conspiracies.

Max sketches the possibilities: if she is there, he will take her in his arms, never mind the sweat, and won't let her go again. She might have gray hair now, wonderful. Or she's put on weight — but Max embraces all change. Married, perhaps, but then anyone can make a mistake. Just as long as she hasn't lost that smile: when her mouth turns down and her eyes narrow completely. Has she brought his child to meet him? A daughter, named Mirafiori, or...

As he approaches First Avenue, Max is increasingly convinced that he is also heading for a pleasant surprise.

He locks onto a black T-shirt and black tights just in front of him. A perfect pacemaker for Max, who can tell she's trained longer than he has. Black is for mourning, or simply to retain heat. She strains with every stride, amidst a riot of thoughts.

* * *

They had had to bury a number of comrades. A., fatal heart attack on a train, in the middle of nowhere, while on his way to see his lover. Montparnasse Cemetery. B., caught defenseless and cut down by the Stasschutz. Zumikon Cemetery, among the financiers in the family plot. C., a hunger strike that reached its illogical conclusion. Others lost their liberty, not their lives: D., twenty years for a bungled robbery. E., implicated in a mass breakout from a women's prison in Italy. F., turned over by the Swiss police to be tortured (electrodes wired to his genitals) in an Istanbul cell. There was a full alphabet of the fallen, down to Fritz Z., also in Zumikon.

European history dictates that the state must not be handed the monopoly on violence. Elections change nothing; at best, they register dissatisfaction with the status quo.

The antinuclear movement imposed the following proof: the balance of forces was first tested on the ground by occupying the sites of the proposed German fast-breeder reactor, as well as the plant outside Basel, stopping work on both. The citizens then gave the go-ahead in a referendum, but the flimsy consensus that emerged made it clear that true legitimacy lay with the movement. Its majority view had won out, with a few sticks of dynamite thrown in for good measure. Everyone, in the end, was indebted to the hardliners, whether as a clear focus for opposition or as a romantic inspiration. This was even true of those who had no vision of the future at all, and that included most of the local politicos.

117

The communiqué claiming responsibility for the blast was unambiguous:

> Ask the thousands of citizens who filed complaints and lodged appeals. They knew injunctions to halt work would be lifted, even before the appeals were heard. The growth of the antinuclear movement is due to the realization by whole sections of society that the nuclear lobby has been flouting the law. But the movement knows that mass demonstrations, such as those at Kalkar, Malville and Gösgen, have their limits. The Nuclear State has given notice that it will no longer tolerate sit-ins and occupations, and is ready to kill — remember Vital Michalon, murdered by the riot police at Malville. That is why it has been decided to pursue our goals through direct action carried out by small, decentralized groups.

The communiqué kept them busy for weeks at the Linguistic Analysis Unit of the so-called security forces.

* * *

After the town cradled in the valley, the plateau swept up again for the last time. He was on an open road, with a clear view of the gentle hills beyond. The moon would rise a bit before four o'clock, but most obstacles were visible by starlight. Tree trunks littered the path here and there, for the woodcutters were taking advantage of the hard ground to drag them to the sawmill. Their tractors left deep frozen ruts in the ground; piles of dry branches awaited the chainsaw or a bonfire. These were risks that had to be run.

The track hugged the spur of the hill, then plunged into the forest, eventually coming to a clearing, suitable for black masses or parachute drops by the Resistance. He granted himself a few minutes rest, under the stars, to eat a bar of chocolate and study the map, his flashlight up close against the paper.

Like orienteering, his mission required military precision to attain its unspoken ends. The enemy was issuing orders from well-appointed offices, while he was gauging the movements of its patrols, ready to change course at a moment's notice. Above all, he could not allow an attack of despondency to interrupt his progress. He folded up the map, wiped some snow from the seat of his pants, then (picturing the plaster cast of his buttocks the forensics experts would make) sat down again, just to the side of the original imprint, widening it. A smile curling up one side of his mouth, he set off again.

The Jura
8 km / 5 miles
Belfort
Hericourt
Montbéliard
Audin
Pont-de-Roide
St Hippolyte
Belleherbe

16
FIRST AVENUE AND 59th STREET

They flee both of them terrified the first one screams calls the other feels a sharp pain in his ear cannot hear anything has a swollen eye unhinged by the shock wave of the explosion then he calls out to him they go a little way about 10 or 15 meters then turn back he moans for a few minutes longer one last loud groan and then there is no sound at all.

Nanni Balestrini, *L'editore*

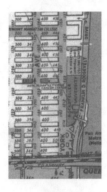

Where Gatsby's beloved Queensboro Bridge starts to slope downwards again, one particularly energetic volunteer, his rubber gloves smeared with a pink goo, offers the marathoners the luxury of a vaseline break. The mix of pollution and sweat causes many — especially the men — to break out in red patches on their inner thighs, under their arms or around their nipples. All they have to do is raise an arm, spread their legs or lift up their shirt as they step up to him, and the "grease monkey" knows just where to apply his obscene jelly. Max's slightly reddening armpits get the treatment, and he's waved off with a grin: Have a nice race!

The blue line follows the ramp down, turns twice to the left and passes under the bridge, next to a factory chimney so tightly woven into the built environment that it cannot safely be demolished, though it has long served no purpose. The bridge usually gives good shelter to the homeless, but their cardboard city was bulldozed away this very morning. For security reasons, quite understandable...

The echo produced in this semi-enclosed space inspires Max to dial up his answering machine and records the sound of thousands of feet, all bound for the longest fully visible straightaway of the course.

As First Avenue heads north it cuts across all the streets from 60th to 125th, to the tip of Manhattan Island, where it crosses the Harlem River to the Bronx via the Willis Avenue Bridge.

Even the most hardened marathoner is likely to choke on first beholding the perspective of these next five miles. Like a telephoto lens, the gradual downhill slope compresses the distance, such that the two sides of the avenue seem to stretch endlessly towards a theoretical point on the horizon where they must converge. Runners in the footsteps of other runners, all within an endless corridor: take it or leave it. The sheer length seems to demand infinite effort, yet promises a magical escape.

As a bonus, the spectators are back — there had been none on the bridge — in row upon tightly packed row, waving flags of many nations and displaying impeccable manners. Crossing one bridge has multiplied the average household income by five. These are the New Yorkers who buy their clothes on Fifth Avenue, wear a different watch every day and seldom clip their own nails, people who wear T-shirts once before giving them to the maid's children, whose trainers don't get scuffed and whose high heels have no damaging encounters with crumbling pavement. Everything is clean to the touch here: balustrades, newspapers that will never become sidewalk litter, money made of paper and plastic: change is what you toss into begging bowls. Skyscrapers are scrubbed clean by robots on automated platforms, water fountains actually work — so fire hydrants can also serve their original purpose — and bus timetables are unobscured by graffiti. No boarded-up storefronts here, no stray garbage bags, no gutted buildings with brambles spilling out of them. You're on Easy Street.

Max is at arm's length from the cheering line of spectators. He can plainly detect all the different scents, on the women mainly — some trick of the wind combined with his own speed, no doubt. Air Du Temps, Lagerfeld? Chanel No. 9, probably. He makes bets with himself. That was Egoïste Pour Homme, or worse. Tomorrow he will put on his tie again; life will flatten out. The women now applauding him will have dispersed, and their perfumes with them. Tomorrow, their smell will be that of the deodorant they roll under their arms.

To all this supply and demand, Max responds with caution and doubt. Now and again he goes into the sports stores along First Avenue to keep up with the latest developments in running-shoe technology. They might have invented something that stops blisters forever, something ultralight and streamlined that never skids when wet. Something waterproof, but which doesn't trap perspiration, or something that absorbs shock but not energy, and provides a rebound without impacting the knee joints. A shoe as fine as a stocking but as sturdy as a mountain boot, neither monochrome nor multicolored; a perfect fit, but not made to measure. Not cheap, and not expensive.

Nike: everyone says nigh-key, but the company points out that the name derives from the Greek goddess of victory and should be pronounced to rhyme with CK, just as famous. Asics already sponsors numerous sporting events, but lead guitarists will eventually step up to the microphone to say Thank you, Adidas! and the Guggenheim will acknowledge that Van Gogh comes to us courtesy of Reebok. Muggers in parks and bullies in schools will as soon take your New Balance trainers as relieve you of your wristwatch or any other badge of fashion.

He'll spend half an hour squeezing soles, pulling laces, disparaging the design, trying on one or two models, and not just any, No, the ones you've got in the window, or These, but do you have them in another color?, and Thanks anyway in the end. The curvature is all wrong, or the leather and canvas combination makes washing a problem, or the big toe isn't supported, there's too much ankle torsion, and anyway the heel's too soft. Unless you're Achilles and make a fetish of running barefoot, every shoe you examine will have a flaw.

The virtual savings he makes allow Max the satisfaction of thinking he has resisted the dictates of mass consumerism — if only out of fear of the new.

The crack in his universe left by Ingeborg's absence would stay with him for a long time. Weekends are the hardest: you have to think up fresh reasons not to smoke, not to lift life a little with a thin white line. But — let's be realistic — it's not complicated: just imagine you are someone who is in love with a dark German woman, and you can't untangle yourself from the memory of her hair next to a bowl of green tea. Obviously, a smoke will not suffice. First you must break the mechanism of dependence and stop blaming the past

week's woes on the want of a cigarette. What spice could a Marlboro add to the featureless life of the office? What use in the pursuit of pleasures that are never quite within reach? He cannot resist, he has to go through all the twists and turns, prove that his existence does not come down to one thing, that he is still the architect of his own life. He would no more be ruled by habit than by the lobby, so on his bedside table he leaves a pack of the same brand they smoked on the tatami in Nagasaki. Finally his fist comes down from a great height and smashes the fantasy, making a terrible noise.

When it comes to smoking, as with the German woman, Max is incapable of cheating directly; but he makes adjustments to the environment. For instance, he has hidden the last cigarette in the recesses of a closet and has willed his memory to lose all track of it.

It's what you call an impasse — best forgotten.

* * *

The houses on the far side of the town were quite grand, and bore all the exterior signs of affluence: patriotic flagpoles on the lawn, plaques denoting property and the illegality of challenging it, garages for cars, bikes, baby carriages. Families of doctors, dentists and executives, held in the sleep of the just, a sleep made possible by tasteful Scandinavian furnishings.

He turned up a street that, according to the sign, would come to a dead end. Just past the final house he picked up the yellow line marking the recommended trail for Sunday hillwalkers, and headed into the forest. The path took him one hundred and fifty meters higher in less than one kilometer, and by the time he reached flatter ground he was flushed with effort and apprehension. He consulted his map, to make sure he didn't miss the next crucial turn. The path became steep again, while the hum of the highway became more distinct. It was right there, below him: his eyes followed each pair of headlights disappearing into, or emerging from, a tunnel. Despite the continuous noise from the road, he proceeded with utmost caution, attentive to the snap of every twig and the rustle of the forest, its hares as nervous as he.

Another level stretch, at the end of which a bench for lovers of nature signaled the continuation of the footpath. It rose steeply to a clearing where a high-tension power pylon had been erected. The air was so dry, or the current so weak, that he could not hear the usual crackle along the wires. Then there was another bench, for lovers, period. Not for him.

* * *

Feltrinelli, the publisher, was the first Italian intellectual to show an interest in high-tension power pylons. Starting in the Sixties, Giangi — short for Giangiacomo — learned about explosives from the how-to manuals of rival publishers. As if other books were of no consequence! Literature was not enough for him, however, nor his trips to Cuba. He wanted to see direct action. Reality on the ground had to be taken into account, and presumably this included the fog — a natural camouflage, but also a hazard — that tends to settle on the Po Valley. The dense humidity can act as a conductor for rogue currents and magnetic fields along power lines; the wires used in electric detonators (if that is what you have opted for) can simultaneously act as induction coils; and if, on top

of that, the explosive charge is in contact with the detonators during the sensitive assembly phase...

The explosion hurled his body against the power pylon, ripping off his legs but leaving his face unscathed. Thus died the man behind the name: Feltrinelli Editore, whose publications, with their distinctive white covers edged in red, were devotedly collected by a whole generation of students at La Statale and La Cattolica. The question as to why Giangi had decided to deprive Milan of its electricity supply on March 18th, 1972, was less compelling than the fact of the gesture itself — the public act of a lone individual, obeying his own call to put aside the weapon of theory and take up the theory of weapons.

They swore on his tomb that they would use only pyrotechnic detonators in future.

17

FIRST AVENUE
AND 75th STREET

She was panting as if her heart would burst.
Then in an ecstasy of heroism, that made her
almost joyous, she ran down the hill, crossed
the cow-plank, the footpath, the alley, the market, and reached the pharmacy.

Gustave Flaubert, *Madame Bovary*

T he blue line is festooned with great
hoops of colored balloons across the full
width of First Avenue. No garbage bags litter
the street, nor even floating pages from the
exceedingly bulky Sunday *New York Times*.
TV crews on motorcycles wend their way
slowly upstream, filming the excited cheers
on one side, the silent struggle on the other.
The street numbers to the left and right of
First Avenue go up, contrary to the countdown along Fourth Avenue in Brooklyn. Both
cut across a variety of cultures and standards
of living.

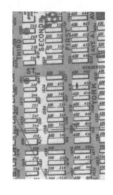

At this level, around 60th Street, store
windows display everything you might need
in the last instance, from champagne to
videos, cosmetics to dry-cleaning.
Apartment buildings aspire to twenty-five,
even fifty stories. Those unable to boast of

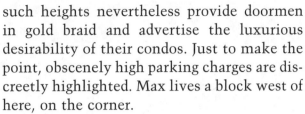

such heights nevertheless provide doormen in gold braid and advertise the luxurious desirability of their condos. Just to make the point, obscenely high parking charges are discreetly highlighted. Max lives a block west of here, on the corner.

First Avenue climbs very gradually until 84th Street, where a Peruvian restaurant, the Monte Carmela, and a sign proclaiming 21,000 VIDEOS IN STOCK mark the crest of the rise. From there the view is all downhill again, the megalopolis stretching away to the far end of Harlem and the Willis Avenue Bridge.

Max locks his gaze onto a head in front of him that is not bobbing up and down, the sign of feet expertly skimming the ground. The book points out that the lift required to raise the forehead two inches per stride adds more than a mile to the distance covered by a marathoner. It also demonstrates the disproportionate effort that results when the legs form an acute rather than a right angle. And that a mere two degrees in the angle formed by the lead leg and the trunk of the body similarly wastes energy.

The man in front of Max is running on the recommended economy setting, but his mouth is so dry that deposits of white spittle have condensed at the corners of his lips.

Max recognizes him.

"John, you got your number!"

"Haven't missed one since '76."

They had met early one chilly morning on the Williamsburg Bridge, after noticing they were both doing the same three-mile practice run on the pedestrian causeway. John has been clocking on for forty years at Con Ed on 43rd Street. He runs on company time whenever he can; his workmates cover for him, page him if necessary. The Con Ed Building does have a gym — down in the basement next to the steam room — with a punching bag to build up the arms, but nothing specially for the legs. John chose the Williamsburg Bridge for training because of its ideal length (which he checked on company surveys) and because its location was unsavory enough to ensure he would never bump into one of the higher-ups from the office.

The two established a kind of rapport, though class and age separated the American, a skilled but still blue-collar worker at 66, from the immigrant, a 49-year-old architect. John told Max about his two lives: the first, married to a Japanese woman, ended with her death from cancer. After the war they'd stayed in Japan for two years, both working for the army. Now, in his second life, his present wife has cancer, as well as being diabetic. She watches TV while he's out training. I keep telling her, running is my chemo. It kills off the bad cells. His second life is coming to an end, too: the chemo hasn't worked.

"How's the job?"

"I'll bet I'm the only one here getting paid by the hour." John points to his pager. "If there's a real emergency the guys at work will page me, and I'll take a taxi. The others are waiting to pick me up at the finish."

John keeps his co-workers abreast of all his preparations for the marathon; he talks of nothing else. They know all about standing in line in the freezing cold the day the first applications are handed out, and about sprinting to the main Manhattan post office to put the form into the special letter box marked MARATHON.

Max has the advantage of a French passport. He gets his number through a travel agent who has a block of reserved places under the overseas quota system (and charges for the privilege). On the other hand, Max's col-

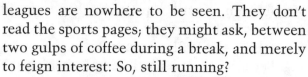

leagues are nowhere to be seen. They don't read the sports pages; they might ask, between two gulps of coffee during a break, and merely to feign interest: So, still running?

So long as he is, it will be alone. Whereas the proletarian has his whole class to run with him.

John's saliva is awfully dry. He's puffing.

"Don't slow down because of me — Go on, it's your first one. I'm shooting for five."

Max doesn't really want to leave him behind.

They go past a knot of runners whom the crowd is acknowledging with a huge cheer. Some are here for their first race, some for their last. Max recognizes the white beard and baseball cap from TV interviews: the man who is synonymous with the New York Marathon, having organized it for the past twenty years, and who is usually in Central Park to greet each finisher personally. This year he publicly announced that he would finish in five hours. He's run more marathons than the years of his life, which are sixty; but the tumors in his brain and thyroid have by now spread to the media, and chemotherapy has left him bald. Cheering spectators point to the fragile silhouette as he goes past: he's the popular favorite, no contest.

The Norwegian woman running beside him is one of the world's great athletes. Not yet forty, she has won dozens of marathons, but this one she's devoting to bringing the local hero safely into home port. Max and John jog alongside for a while, and would shout out words of encouragement, but the pain and strain etched so deeply in his face move them to silence.

Max wishes John and the proletariat good luck, and moves on.

* * *

They were their own worst enemies, on intimate terms with the adversary within. They fought themselves, their upbringing, the moral code inherited from their racist, nationalist, middle-class environment.

They went on every kind of protest, especially the more violent ones, wearing balaclavas to make the job of the lobby's photographers more difficult. They stood up to rubber bullets at point-blank range, truncheons to the skull and body blows with riot shields; they wiped the tear gas from their eyes as they surged forward and back around the nuclear plant site; they put up barricades, covered their faces with bandannas, met in disused quarries to practice the correct way of throwing Molotov cocktails: arms outstretched so you don't set fire to your clothes. They learned how to handle guns at shooting ranges, places where security guards and the dregs of the police force tended to hang out. They honed their urban guerrilla tactics and prepared for all-out war by storing chlorate (in the form of weed-killer) and sulfuric acid in a cache on the edge of town. They studied history, not the history of generals but of peasant heroes, urban outlaws, the Bonnot gang, Giangi and the new partisans.

* * *

He walked quickly and warily through the streets of the town, watchful behind the mask, which impeded his breathing. Any unwelcome inquiry would be met with a rambling drunken story about coming home from the carnival disguised as the son of William Tell. The town was stubbornly deserted, however; the real revelers, having hung up their masks, were sleeping off the champagne, and it was still some hours before the first beer.

There were two unavoidable crossings, the river and the railway line, but either could be negotiated at different points. He chose the shortest route.

Mist rose like inconsequential smoke off the river. The crossing was so narrow that he barely had time to jettison the wrapping for the black pepper which he had scattered as a precaution against police dogs. He watched the empty paper cone fill with water and sink.

Under the railway bridge, the echo of his steps alarmed him: surely he was going too fast to give credence to the carnival story. Rather than slow his pace, he speeded up again. Better to be out of here as quickly as possible, where his footfalls would not resonate.

Two church steeples, two clocks: they confirmed that he still faced long hours of endurance before he could settle into the warmth of a predetermined train. He wondered if the gods who protected the lone warrior would continue to look down on him with benevolence.

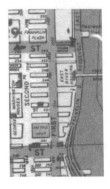

18
FIRST AVENUE
AND 95th STREET

Ah! Why go on running? — Better to wait there, leaning against a tree. Better to give up Switzerland and the illusion. Give up being free, give up women. Freedom includes being able to sleep with a woman. What awaited me was the retaliation camp. Ah! God damn it, no! Ah! I could not give up! I would gallop straight ahead until I fell down, until I died!
I sped headlong into the night, knocking against the trunks of the birch trees: startled by the dull thud of clumps of snow as they slid from the branches.

Emmanuel Roblès, *Erica*

They are not the only ones kept out of the running. First Avenue is usually prime begging territory for the homeless, who have been cleared out for a day. You recognize them, as winter nears, from their hoods, which they never take off. Indefatigable behind shopping carts filled with plastic bags and paper — but somehow there's always room for more — they spend their days accumulating wrapping of all types: the indispensable insulation, added layers at a time as the temperature drops, among which hats, caps, hoods and gloves are the prize items. By Christmas time, only a few inches of skin are exposed to the elements. What does show is

so caked with dirt you can't always tell black from white, male from female. A cup for people to put coins in is also required, as well as all the stuff that goes to make up a windproof bed: corrugated cardboard, magazines, white polystyrene boxes from the fish market, torn curtains, American flags.

In Max's mother tongue they are called sans-abris — the unsheltered. But in English and in New York, a hundred thousand or so are literally home-less: the word contains your TV, toaster and fridge, and the elegant leather couch from which you can admire them.

Max knows precisely where the hooded people are to be found: under awnings, on public benches, in any number of recesses built into the urban terrain. They are a permanent foil to his solitude within the system. If you don't make yourself useful, you could end up like them. Today you're running down First Avenue, but tomorrow you could be left behind and left out — permanently disqualified. Swathed in newsprint.

All the more reason to make the sacrifice, in the flesh, and face the Wall — to run to the very limit of what can be endured. Like the first women who ran the Olympic marathon in 1984.

* * *

At the time, the papers spoke not of the Vendôme Column or the Communards who demolished it, but of another symbolic monument. According to one,

An explosion ripped through the "Lügenpavillon" ("Disinformation Center") — during the night of February 19th-20th, on the evening of the referendum on the so-called antinuclear proposition, which was rejected by 965,927 votes to 920,480.

And another:

Following the failure of yesterday's referendum on the nuclear question, the information center at the construction site of the K*** plant has been destroyed by a powerful incendiary device in an overnight attack. Only the structure's metal frame was left standing. There were no casualties, but damage to the site is estimated at four million francs. Signs warning of the explosion were found placed along the road that leads to the center.

The voters that day appeared to have disavowed the movement, by a whisker. But another referendum a few years later reversed the decision, and the K*** project was abandoned once and for all. A triumph for propaganda through action, in keeping with the Jura's long tradition in this obstinate land.

★ ★ ★

Leaving one village behind on this, the initial upward sweep of the Jura, he came to the edge of a forest, from where he could see the thousand lights of the town in the valley, illuminating its streets, schools and church steeples, the train station and the tavern signs. The fugitive (his body weight pitched forward, onto his front thighs) felt sure that the town would be fast asleep nonetheless.

At this altitude the snow had already melted, but he remained wary of icy patches that might remain. He skirted around a coun-

try inn (Visit Our Panoramic Terrace) and picked up a path much used by weekend walkers to admire the south-facing gardens of a row of villas. A group of figures — seven dwarves in a ring around Snow White — presided over a miniature eco-habitat; tiny chalets, dotted around a drained pool, represented the diversity of the fatherland. From the age of the trees, he could tell that this area was the preserve of an older generation of *nouveaux riches.*

He took from his pocket a rubber mask of a child's face, topped by an apple with an arrow through it, with which he would meet the gaze of any curious passerby in the streets of the town. It restricted his breathing at first, and proved unnecessary in any case, as there was no one about to point and laugh. The ice on the car windows in front of the police station showed they had not been moved all night, but there was one empty space between two of the cars, and a light shone from somewhere on the first floor. A burst of speed made the apple bob pointlessly above his head; the crossbow would be safely locked away in the police armory.

19

FIRST AVENUE
AND 115th STREET

In the beginning I would get quickly out of
breath and take frequent breaks (not yet being
practiced in this new skill of inscribing my
body on the fabric of the world), pausing repeatedly to walk, since I had decided deep down
that never again would I force myself. But now
I can run all in one go, almost effortlessly, from
the Vidy Theater to the little bridge over the
Vaudaire, with a smooth and supple stride, my
heart beating to the cadence of the earth, the
earth that gives me energy and support, that
gently pushes me forward and holds me back.

Silvia Ricci Lempen, *Un homme tragique*

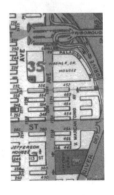

T he pain of running, the Wall still lying in
wait, and no sign yet of the kids of Harlem.

After the Peruvian restaurant where First
Avenue peaks, the social makeup of the crowd
begins to change. The Isaac Homes tower
blocks rise to fifty stories, like the buildings at
60th Street, but they are distinctly more modest, with no stores or window displays at
street level. As the buildings grow smaller,
skins grow darker, and the blue line enters
Spanish Harlem. El Barrio.

At 92nd, on the left, the first vacant lot
makes its appearance. It has been taken over
by a profusion of weeds and secured behind a
high, plain wire fence — barbs not yet needed.

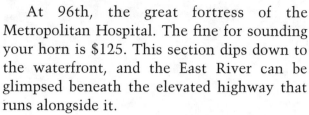

At 96th, the great fortress of the Metropolitan Hospital. The fine for sounding your horn is $125. This section dips down to the waterfront, and the East River can be glimpsed beneath the elevated highway that runs alongside it.

Security cameras monitor a vast parking lot filled with row upon tidy row of white vehicles, all daubed with graffiti, that serve the city roadworks department. They, too, must have a day of rest.

At 103rd, another vacant lot. Unfenced, it has become a general garbage dump. Further on, used cars, trucks and mobile homes for sale, credit cards not accepted. With every stride, Wall Street recedes further into the distance.

Starting at 105th, Pentecostal churches and scorched buildings.

By 110th Street, half the buildings are derelict and unoccupied. Storefront blinds are permanently lowered; business is now done on the sidewalk, amid heaped goods of indeterminate origin. This is the dark side of First Avenue.

"There, I've finished!" says the voice in his headband. Out of nowhere: Max hears no sound of a connection being made this time. Like a child's cry in a stairwell, excited, genuine. Max cannot contain himself:

"What have you finished, Ingeborg?"

"In two hours fifty-nine. Thanks to my wheelchair — really low off the ground."

Max chokes, cannot manage more than two breaths out for each breath in.

Ingeborg paralyzed — as they had predicted, after the bomb, at her birth... The shock robs him of what little oxygen the race still allowed him. Her hair often obscured her eyes. Her name concealed her origins. Her absence made the facts vague. She wore supports in her shoes to correct a slight limp.

In the hotel room in Nagasaki, they had talked about what might happen if the problem with her hips recurred. I'll hide, she had sworn. No one will find me. Ingeborg always keeps her word. She will not let herself (her self) be stripped bare.

At the Verrazano-Narrows Bridge he had noticed the wheelchair marathoners at their starting line. They put bandages on their thumbs, under their gloves: that's where they'll be hurting. He only saw them from the back; what if he had recognized an Asian silhouette? Of the twenty-five thousand people who cross New York — breathless — once a year, how many know each other, and how many of those will meet on the day? Max had found Bernard K.'s name on the list — he is now a cabinet minister — but it hadn't occurred to him to look for Ingeborg.

A man of fifty and his crippled love: each, on their own, trying to find the thread, the guideline. And it is blue. But they couldn't have done it together. Wheelchairs go too fast on the downhills. They have a wider turning angle. And the whole approach to rehydration is different.

"Under three hours — is it your first marathon?"

"Yours too, isn't it, Max?"

"You amaze me."

And as soon as the words are spoken into the microphone, he knows they bring bad news.

"Max, can we talk about Nagasaki for a minute?"

"But, Ingeborg, we're going to see each other when I finish. We could –"

"No, there's a bus for wheelchair users, and I've got to catch a flight to Japan."

"I want to see you, damn it!"

She does not answer. His fear is that she

will hang up and he'll lose it all. Left with nothing to negotiate. Then:

"Listen, Max, I know you're in charge of the Nagasaki cargo terminal. They were afraid the opposition would turn violent, so they chose your firm. That way it would all be managed from the States. Okay, I know you're on the technical side. But that airport is going to be used to rebuild the Japanese air force. And what's more, they want to put a runway through a cemetery, a cemetery for victims of the bomb! You must know that."

Max is silent. Yes, he's aware of the situation. The airport in question is, from his perspective, a mere topic for study, having neither weight nor mass: a paper concept, money in a memory bank. Sketches, proposals, final blueprints. The neutrality of technology, recorded on paper and stored in filing cabinets. Something you approach from the outside, many time zones away.

"You've got to give me the plans, the names of all the companies involved, the timetable. That airport is not going to be built."

She talks in bullets, the staccato intonation that earned her a Germanic alias. Nothing disabled about it, much less the voice of someone who's just finished a marathon.

What she wants is as clear and calculated as the language of Greenwar — the lobby's own language, used to engineer its downfall. All over the planet, the green knights of the whirlwind mount their improbable deeds and bring them off through sheer determination. One after another, a building site is bombed, a barracks goes up in smoke, a runway is damaged, a nuclear test sabotaged, a satellite nudged out of orbit. The message is plain: when Greenwar scores, the lobby retreats.

"Max, are you listening?"

"Yes. But how do I know you're in Central

Park and not in front of your television in Nagasaki, watching the marathon in the middle of the night? There's no proof this isn't another one of your stunts."

"So we have to have proof now, you and I? And what were you doing, Max, on that cold night in February?"

She hangs up, ending her fourth call.

Dazed, Max is left staring at a gigantic billboard, an anti-smoking message in which a black child is saying First they made us plant it, now they want us to smoke it. A whiff of anti-white racism on First Avenue above 110th Street... or just a basic revulsion against slavery? In the Hispanic part of Harlem, the advertisements are in Spanish; Coke sells in any and every language. Mexican beer is depicted on billboards with a fuse in the bottle, like a Molotov cocktail: The Spark That Ignites Your Thirst.

Harlem, a Dutch name as plump as a tulip. How many of those now following the blue line into this district would go there alone? Who among the Americans and foreigners here for an expensive and privileged weekend would dare join Max on a weekday practice run in this neighborhood, where he has to dodge dozy yellow cabs by outrunning them? On arrival from Europe fifteen years ago, he quickly got used to drawing mental barbed wire around particular names on the map; Harlem and South Bronx meant ghetto, that is to say, virtually inaccessible, although crossable by subway or taxi.

His perception has changed since he began training for the marathon, however. Not a lot can happen to the solitary individual, almost naked, obviously carrying no money or valuables or food stamps, who chugs along above 100th Street in the early morning. He is momentarily in a state of near-total destitu-

tion, after all, so there would be little point in threatening him with a switchblade or a hypodermic full of supposedly HIV-positive blood. He could always be taken and held for ransom, but that presupposes a degree of organization not usually within the capabilities of kids looking to score some easy crack. And given he's an athlete, he might be able to defend himself. He might be into martial arts.

For a member of society's elite to cross Harlem like this could also be interpreted as an act of provocation, leading logically to the occasional stray bottle hurled at the arrogant skull. Like thousands of others, Max's first training circuit is the sanitized corridor along the East River waterfront, between 61st Street and the Willis Avenue Bridge. It's been "made safe" for whites — in other words, it's swarming with cops. One day, Max decides to break his self-imposed isolation; he chooses a Sunday, when busloads of tourists would be escorted into the churches of Harlem to hear blues and gospel, then shepherded out again for immediate evacuation.

The trial run goes well. No one curses him from an unknown window, no bullets ricochet at his feet. A few jokers join in, following close on his heels, laughing; one kid asks him for his autograph. Together they gain speed, right up to the invisible line that marks the end of their territory, then fall back in good order. Max continues zapping from one block to the next, so naturally that in the end nobody pays him any mind, not even the blue air-conditioned cruisers, all sirens, flashing lights and .22s at the ready.

The city belongs to those who run through it...

Thousands run through Harlem with him today, but today the streets ring with applause. Women of vast girth and the booming voices of gospel singers are hooting at the sight of an unpleasingly skinny female. "Honey, you better get yourself something to eat at the end!" And they burst into laughter again.

★ ★ ★

They admired Giangiacomo.

In 1942, at the age of sixteen, he joined the Communist underground in Milan, and welcomed the American armed forces as they pushed north in the liberation of Italy.

At twenty he was part of the intelligence network set up by former partisans to keep an eye on the household of the ex-king and his mother, newly remarried. It was he who gave L'Unità the sensational scoop that Umberto II was planning a coup d'état if the constitutional referendum went against the monarchy. The son of one of the wealthiest families in the country was using his privileged position to denounce his own class.

In the wake of the assassination attempt on Togliatti, he was sent to jail for putting up posters calling for violent protest. At twenty-two he set up the Feltrinelli Institute for the study of the working class.

In 1954 he launched his own publishing venture with all the savvy of a seasoned capitalist. He was twenty-eight years old. Within two years he had published Doctor Zhivago, thanks to his contacts among the Russian dissidents. His relations with the Stalinist wing of the Communist Party never recovered.

In 1964 he went to Cuba and met Che Guevara, who was to die under torture three years later in Bolivia. Giangiacomo's response was to form the Partisan Action Groups. The liquidation in Hamburg of Quintanilla, Che's executioner, would be their most successful operation.

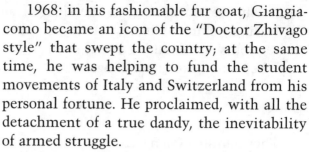

1968: in his fashionable fur coat, Giangiacomo became an icon of the "Doctor Zhivago style" that swept the country; at the same time, he was helping to fund the student movements of Italy and Switzerland from his personal fortune. He proclaimed, with all the detachment of a true dandy, the inevitability of armed struggle.

While in Uruguay in 1971, he made contact with the Tupamaros, who had just raided the armory of the local Swiss community's gun club. Back in Europe, he published texts by and about South American revolutionary movements.

Capitalizing on the fame of his publishing business, he successfully launched a chain of bookstores. While browsing in his shops, they met others of their persuasion; after reading his books, they joined the new partisan groups, the Red Brigades or the autonomous movement.

The decision to go underground sprang from his conviction that Italy was heading for a right-wing coup that would usher in the sort of dictatorship that blighted Greece, Spain and Portugal. But he was better suited to spying on the worldwide ruling class than planting bombs, and so he ended up blown to bits under a still-standing pylon. He knew all about books, and not enough about detonators. In praise of arms, he lost his legs.

After all that, they owed him a dedication.

* * *

He could see a stream of headlights, several kilometers away, emerging from a tunnel: part of the north-south flow of traffic across Europe, in all seasons and weathers. No sound from the highway, or indeed from the town, reached his ears. He was running, with a smooth, even stride, along a hillside whose terraced vineyards overlooked the wholly urbanized valley.

He was alert to the danger of twisting his ankle on a loose stone in his path; any such accident would leave him at the mercy of the lobby. That is why there were painkillers in his pocket, but with any luck he would not have to use them.

He needed to find a flight of steps cut into the hillside, leading down through the vineyards, as indicated on the map, but missed the turn and had to go back. Panicking, he took out the flashlight, cursing, and threw a stone high over the vines. Its landing was barely audible, which gave him heart. Finally he reached the patio of a restaurant, the sort that sells beef and rabbit in bulk quantities. At this point he had no alternative but to pass between two buildings: not that it came as a surprise, but the danger was real. He stopped, listened hard to the silence, caught his breath. And threw himself forward.

The way was clear. Afterwards, his heart continued to pound crazily in his chest with the terror of everything that had not happened.

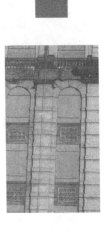

20
WILLIS AVENUE BRIDGE

There are people of all ages — lots of middle-aged people, as well as the elderly. Most are not dreaming of some victory, bereft as they are of any great athletic ambition. It is just taking part in something, doing their bit, conquering themselves. None of which I would underestimate in any way. I can even see myself in their shoes, doing the best I could. But I know I wouldn't make it. Would I take part if I had a chance of succeeding? I don't know. No point in agonizing over the question, since in any case you have no chance of success if you don't take part.

I was told it was something you had to see. You watch them go by, drained and haggard, with wrenched faces, lumbering on hobbled feet, suffering, dying of thirst, sweating and gasping. Those who said I should go and see for myself think the whole spectacle is absurd; they shake their heads and shrug.

Peter Bichsel, *Geschichten zur falschen Zeit*

Willis Avenue Bridge — another one partially closed for repairs — has just one lane that can safely accommodate the blue line. (Radical ecologists think the city should simply let all Manhattan's road bridges rot away, and instead provide footbridges for bikes and pedestrians.) The turbid waters of Harlem River are visible below, through the steel meshwork; a narrow strip of synthetic carpet has been laid down for the occasion. To the right, the Triborough Bridge. Three more to the left: Third Avenue, then a railroad bridge, then Madison Avenue, along which a procession of wingless ants is making its way out of the Bronx.

The zone spanned by the bridge once it has cleared the water is green, but it is the green of desolation: railroad tracks taken over by weeds and thorns. On either side, some twenty brick apartment blocks, rising to forty stories; in the foreground, burnt-out shells of buildings. In the Bronx, green is always a bad omen, signaling abandonment of the human to the vegetable — abandonment, period.

The first building by the bridge serves only one purpose, to hold up a gigantic advertising sign (WHY PAY MORE?). Its windows are bricked up all the way to the sixth floor. The flat tarred roof of the next building has trapped an assortment of beer bottles, Coke cans and other missiles thrown from the windows of passing cars.

Civilized order eventually takes over again; on the left, high-rises are a sign of progress, even if all their apertures have been barred and their lighting smashed by vandals. On the right, though, the old order persists — houses whose windowpanes have been replaced with cardboard or corrugated iron, or not at all. Renovation is not on the cards; decay and fire and bulldozers must be. The people who live in these hovels are not on any voting lists and don't elect the President.

When he sets himself a specific goal, Max does not expect to fail. He is built to win — as long as nothing gives way, and his knees hold, and his breathing, and that passionate faculty known as the will, whose true location has never been found.

For some — those with no known enemies — it becomes a race against themselves, a variation on the Protestant work ethic. But the "conquest of the self" and its implicit schizo-

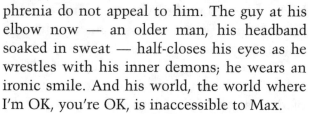

phrenia do not appeal to him. The guy at his elbow now — an older man, his headband soaked in sweat — half-closes his eyes as he wrestles with his inner demons; he wears an ironic smile. And his world, the world where I'm OK, you're OK, is inaccessible to Max.

Hug the blue line. Think about what is behind you. Don't say to yourself: six miles to go, maybe worse. How many? He has to start over twice — a symptom of drought in the brain. Blood is flowing to the legs instead. A sudden raised section of pavement: one more hazard. The heel comes down awkwardly, bingo, you've twisted your ankle. How many times does the heel hit the pavement? Say, three feet per stride. Which, if you divide by... makes...

But the blood isn't reaching his head at all: it is all rushing to a pain in his hip.

If the proposition is that, as he runs, Max is following two lines — the one that takes him from the first to the twenty-sixth mile in four hours, and the one that moves backwards, from end to beginning, through the past of an eco-warrior — then the missing element (the justification of the present, the threads that connect him to the future) would be the German woman.

Max is a reservist in the green brigades. When the *New York Times* reports the latest exploit of the eco-fundamentalists, he rejoices: Another point scored against the lobby. Reading the statement that claims responsibility for the latest outrage, he thinks: This is the true literature of our times. He admires Greenwar, the armed wing of the environmental struggle, for its assault on the symbols and images of power, but never on people. Max (unlike many) has taken a good hard look at the Eastern bloc as it crumbled, and at Vladimir Illich, as they removed him from

Red Square; he's observed the holes in the ozone layer and the sundry manifestations of smog, and noted how many patents have been taken out against life, against species, against diversity. He has come to the conclusion that the time has come. Time to expose the lobby, to chuck fistfuls of dreams into its delicate machinery.

So, it is you and I who make history. Max, going back to his roots, in the planet. He is the planet; he soars above it. At nearly fifty, in the midst of a marathon, the gauntlet is thrown down. Even if you haven't brought down the Vendôme column, like Gustave. What will he say to Ingeborg?

They loved Feltrinelli's nearsightedness behind the tortoise-shell frames, his trendy mustache, the cashmere sweater over his white shirt. His trim figure was that of the well-born, his cigarettes those of the working class. The photograph of Giangi on the front page of Potere Operaio, dated March 26th, 1972, long hung on the walls of their smoke-filled rooms. The short hair, the troubled smile, the final farewell printed in tall red capital letters. Was it possible, even in this latest exile, not to resemble him?

The 1980s were a decade weighed down by the defeatism of the post-modernists and the opportunism of the left (and the rest). Its novels dripped with ennui, fine writing and the confessional tone of those who have repented of life. But the end of the century must also spell the end of the New Realism. Giangi's back in town, lock up your generators. Never mind jet lag, this is the hour of reckoning. And when is it all expected to blow up? asks the anchorwoman in her soothing voice.

It is all too easy to describe anything lasting longer than usual as a marathon, be it a legislative session, a dance contest, a film.

Nicolas de Stael gave the title Marathon to one of his paintings, an obviously laborious piece that hangs in the Tate Gallery. Such comparisons have but one flaw: they leave out the Wall.

At about the twentieth mile, the runner reaches a physiological limit which can be measured. Regardless of fitness, regardless of training, and however strong the walls of the heart itself — there is a threshold that, once reached, forces a change in the energy supply as normal reserves drop to zero. The brain's chemistry is flooded with contradictory messages, some demanding an immediate halt, others leading to a state of detachment, in which the Wall may be seen from above. Only this detachment can get you over it. Or around it, which is even better.

Max has come up against it more than once in his training. Willpower and brute strength are to no avail. The legs drag, despair rises from the thighs and overwhelms all thought. Once the mind has been left behind by the body, it can make excuses for its companion, but that is as far as it goes. You have to get to somewhere that is outside both mind and body.

You see yourself from afar, from overhead, as if in a mirror at the side of the road, drawing strength from the separation of the subject and its pain. The marathon, as Sartre remarked of the novel, is "a short induced neurosis."

So near his goal, yet Max is exhausted, cold sweat drenching his socks. This is not a team sport.

The spectators — your last companions — are beyond reach. Never mind the crowds, never mind Gandhi, Jesus, Mao and their respective long marches. Agreed, the human body was not made for sitting, but neither was it made to run without pause. You can die from it.

Mexico City, 1912: Tom Longboat, an Amerindian, resuscitates a fellow runner's stopped heart by smacking his chest half a dozen times.

The last twenty per cent consumes eighty per cent of the resources. The disproportion is grotesque, but the race doesn't have to make sense to be enjoyed.

Sense. En-joyed.

So short of breath. Thoughts of one syllable only. Symptoms nearly gone. A calm that observes each arduous beat of the heart. Reasoning flags. Synthetic. Dreams. If this stage... endured... runner entering... Runner's high. His drug, his ecstasy. Marathon orgasm.

Whisper. Wall.

* * *

After the initial slope that climbs up from the Rhine, he came to the first village, which afforded the option of an escape — in case injury or exhaustion ruled out proceeding any further. He would await a mail van that was scheduled to stop in the village at six-thirty. Now, at three o'clock in the morning, he was jogging past the stop and smiling in the knowledge that it would not be needed.

Leaving the village, he veered immediately to the right. The forest would provide cover during the next gradual ascent, over a distance of some two kilometers. This section of the route (planned with the precision of a motor rally) was the easiest: a neat, well-tended path through a cultivated stand of evergreens. Like a cross-country trail in Finland. No ice or snow, no unwelcome encounters. He could have sprinted the distance, as if on an asphalt track.

Every hundred yards or so, wood had been carefully stacked in piles and left to dry

before being carted off to burn in fireplaces of which he knew nothing. He breathed in the characteristic scent of Mediterranean pine as he passed by; speeding up, he felt the urge to raise his arms up high, like a runner completing some extraordinary achievement, in a kind of ecstasy.

A continuous sound, of which he was at first only dimly aware, grew more distinct. He stopped dead. A suspicious purring noise that he set his mind to analyzing, forcing his brain to exercise more strenuously than his legs. One by one he reviewed all possible catastrophic scenarios, until he found the explanation. It was an electric generator, powering a nearby radio mast.

He set off again, on his merry way.

21
FIFTH AVENUE
AND 137th STREET

> I ran to a steady jog-trot rhythm, and soon it
> was so smooth that I forgot I was running, and
> I was hardly able to know that my legs were lift-
> ing and falling and my arms going in and out,
> and my lungs didn't seem to be working at all,
> and my heart stopped that wicked thumping I
> always get at the beginning of a run. Because
> you see I never race at all; I just run, and some-
> how I know that if I forget I'm racing and only
> jog-trot along until I don't know I'm running I
> always win the race.
>
> Alan Sillitoe, *The Loneliness*
> *of the Long-Distance Runner*

At the side of the road, right in front of
40th Precinct headquarters, are the rust-
ing carcasses of two burnt-out automobiles. It
looks like a movie set, but it's just the banal
reality of the South Bronx.

The roof of the 40th is equipped with huge
antennas for calling in the troops in case of
rioting. Old Glory flutters over the entrance.
The proud fleet of blue and white Chryslers,
with their red and white flashing lights, are
well matched with their drivers, in their blue
caps and blue short-sleeved shirts, who
munch on chicken sandwiches with the
motor idling. Crime doesn't pay.

It was the same kind of police station,
though more modern, in the north German

city where Quintanilla was liquidated by the German woman. The cops held the line behind their transparent shields; the water cannon had been brought forward; the protesters were ordered to disperse. A bandanna over her mouth and nose made her unrecognizable. She had a lemon in her pocket (for the tear gas) and steel ball bearings in her belt, to shatter the lobby's windows. The Feldmarschall of the mounted police spat his ultimatum through a megaphone. They were taking over the street, reclaiming it — as if the reign of the internal combustion engine had come to an end. This is your final warning!

It takes some nerve to bring a caravan of healthy, right-thinking, well-nourished non-smokers and non-addicts into this environment, although after twenty miles they may feel a kinship with the people who inhabit this godforsaken place. The difference is that the marathoners leave again within hours, while the heroin addicts remain, and tend to multiply. The column of ants, watched over by helicopters, might just as well be oblivious of its surroundings.

This warscape — its only livable spaces the basements of ruined buildings — is thick with police, who have largely replaced the public. They are posted every ten yards, standing by their motorcycles or sitting in their cars. The race files by in eerie silence. Just here and there, a ripple of (ironic) applause, a smart comment. Got change for a dollar, man?

Max came here, once, to train. At top speed. Taking care not to slow down in front of a particularly animated group of dealers, and to avoid the flailing arms of the half-crazed wretches reaching out to grab at anything that moves. What's frightening is not the black color of skin but the abasement of the person, and the absence of community.

The Hassidic Jews similarly turned their backs on the race, but they at least were talking to one another. They have other interests. No one in this part of the South Bronx is interested in anything, neither in the marathon nor in some lone figure on the sidewalk jabbering to himself.

The blue line takes fright as well. Hardly has it entered the Bronx over the Willis Avenue Bridge than it turns twice and leaves the island again, heading for Madison Avenue and 135th Street.

Over the next few years, this area will be given a makeover. The selection process has begun, and the prospective residents of a cluster of forty-story brick buildings are already being interviewed. Until then, however, the organizing committee is seriously thinking of modifying this part of the blue line's itinerary.

* * *

He stopped before the first village for the ritual farewell. Stripping down to his underwear and the dripping-wet shirt that stuck to his skin, he changed every item of clothing in a well-rehearsed sequence. Not forgetting the carnival mask, a hideous toad face. Methodically, the old never touching the new: the forensic labs and their electron microscopes would have sweet nothing to report. No pang of regret accompanied the passing, for each item of clothing was anonymous. No labels or laundry marks. Either brand-new, or artificially worn: his shoes, for example, had been filed down at the heel to produce a misleading picture of the runner's foot.

Still with the headlamp on, he came to the final operation: changing gloves. Then he doused the pile with the contents of a bottle. The pants soaked up the fluid; he lit a match. An act of arson that (for once) he could stay and watch. As the fire danced, he ate a grape-sugar candy, a cereal bar and half his ration of tea. The soles proved especially flame-resistant.

He used a stick to push the remains into the river and headed off towards the village, making a final adjustment to the repulsive plastic disguise. Bending forwards to mimic old age, he limped spryly past a few sleeping farms and soon came unavoidably within full view of the rifle club and its cafe. Other than the sound of wine-drenched hymns to the fatherland, nothing and no one emerged into the night air. The old toad hopped on into the forest. A little further and he ditched the now superfluous mask. It was going according to plan.

* * *

He was crossing the Jura in the same direction as Gustave Courbet, who had also followed his own inclination, leaving behind him as he climbed the ruins of the Vendôme Column. The people of the Paris Commune had applauded it, but could this work of destruction really be ascribed to Courbet? Perhaps it was because, as a citizen, he had refused the Legion of Honor, or because he was both a friend of Proudhon and president of the Society of Artists. Rather than go to prison, as in 1871, he chose exile.

His hurried escape began in Ornans, at the foot of the Jura. We learn from his later correspondence that he lost his glasses at one point, and kept forgetting to wind up his watch. He ascended from the Loue River to a little-used mountain pass in successive stages, passing through villages along the road and from the plane trees of the lowlands to the conifers of the ridge crest overlooking the

lakes, all the while outwitting the French gendarmes (with the help of friends who prepared
each stage of the journey). Once in
Switzerland, he settled on the far side of the
great lake and stayed there until his death.

One of Gustave's only sculptures is of Free
Helvetia, modeled after Madame Arnaud de
l'Ariège, a former chatelaine who had become
a republican. He donated it to La Tour-de-
Peilz, the village which had given him asylum, for the church fountain.

Gustave's boyhood friend from Ornans, the
socialist writer Max Buchon, had also been
forced to flee France in a previous coup d'état,
on December 2nd, 1851. Gustave often visited
Max in his Bern exile, and the strength of their
friendship, judging by their letters to one
another, was as solid as a Jura fir.

Every escape resembles every other.

22
FIFTH AVENUE AND
120th STREET

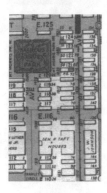

And they all ran down the strand to see over
the houses and the church, helterskelter [...]
— Come on, Gerty, Cissy called. It's the
bazaar fireworks.
But Gerty was adamant. She had no inten-
tion of being at their beck and call. If they
could run like rossies she could sit so she said
she could see from where she was. [...]
She walked with a certain quiet dignity
characteristic of her but with care and very
slowly because — because Gerty MacDowell
was ...
Tight boots? No. She's lame! O!
Mr Bloom watched her as she limped away.
Poor girl! That's why she's left on the shelf and
the others did a sprint. Thought something
was wrong by the cut of her jib. Jilted Beauty.
A defect is ten times worse in a woman.

James Joyce, *Ulysses*

Max is in Dublin to do a feasibility study
for the enlargement of an air cargo terminal. Mornings devoted to working sessions;
a few books packed in his suitcase for after. He
intends to find out why, in 1904, James Joyce
left Dublin for the Continent. A map indicates
the location of the Martello tower on the sea,
just to the south of the city, where Joyce had
taken refuge. The English built many such
coastal fortifications against the expected
invasion by Napoleon and his troops.

On the night of September 14th, 1904, Joyce and his friends, Gogarty and Trench, are asleep in the tower. Trench has a drunken nightmare in which there is a panther in the fireplace. Half asleep, he seizes a rifle and fires into the air to frighten the beast, then goes back to bed. Gogarty takes the rifle off him, swearing it is he who will take care of any animals, and empties a full load into the soup tureen just above Joyce's head. The writer leaps up, dresses, flees from the tower and returns to Dublin in the dead of night. When they open the doors of the National Library next morning, he is there, waiting.

Joyce never returned to the tower, and left Ireland for good a few days later, taking his wife Nora with him to Trieste. Max's admiration trails in his posthumous wake, for he respects (and emulates) the immigrant who never looks back.

Shots in the air — not quite a cannon blast at Verrazano Bridge — and Joyce makes his escape. As writers must.

New York in November. A cloudless sky of cool, serene blue. This used to be an Irish neighborhood.

Max's thoughts take him back to Dublin. He has long believed that it was on his mad race to the library that Joyce conceived of Ulysses. A literary theory that Max alone can fathom, having run the same distance. Joyce must have thought he was going to die; did it take a whole body of work to recover from one moment of fear? All his life, he could hear the rifle blast in the soup tureen — but he lived to tell the tale, and transposed it to June 16th, 1904, the day he first made love to Nora. Joyce's part is played by Leopold Bloom, and Ulysses opens in the tower, on the morning of Bloomsday.

Max runs Joyce's escape route in reverse, as is often the case with memories of flight.

From the centre of Dublin, along the dark sea, to his destination. In his track suit, not even winded, at dawn: Max slows down as he approaches the tower on Forty Foot Beach. There's an inscription on a rock, For Gentlemen Only... Since 1880. He does his halfway stretching exercises as a man nearby strips off and plunges into the icy water. A naked Irishman knows no season.

So, James, how could it have taken you all night to get from the tower to Dublin, arriving at opening time — which happens to be ten o'clock — in front of the National Library? With all due respect, that's only ten miles. Max does it in an hour and a half, and expects to do the round trip in three hours. Which gives him just enough time to shower before the first meeting of the day.

The seasons come earlier here than on the Continent: there are flowers everywhere, even in the buttonholes of the passers-by. Cherry blossom glimpsed in the lush gardens of the embassies — the Japanese apple tree, here on Irish soil. This part of the city is heavily defended by the police, but not against IRA terrorists. Against the ranks of the jobless, the homeless, the foodless who haven't managed to emigrate. Against the dignity-less, the ones who might lie down to sleep in your flower bed; but you have only to give them a steely look and say, Get out! and they skedaddle, like schoolkids running from the truant officer.

The weather changes suddenly on this island. Max's glasses stream with rain, then the sun dazzles the sea, then dense cloud returns, bringing a wind that seeks to thwart all his efforts and two layers of T-shirt. He stops at a gas station to ask for water, as he's been running dry for two hours. The attendant doesn't grasp that he's on foot and hands him a watering can for his overheated motor. Eventually, a dialogue ensues. The New York City marathon! And would it be every day you're training? Will you not go to sleep now, once you're home? Do they pay you to do this at all?

Max doesn't mention James, a writer genuinely loved by the people. The gas station attendant would think he was crazy to run someone else's race. Competing with a national hero!

The run from Sandygrove as Max hones his theory: the odyssey, not of Leopold Bloom, but of Joyce fleeing in the night from the drunken nightmares of his trigger-happy companions. Stray dogs scavenge along the beach as Max, still pursuing James, steps in slippery seaweed left by the low tide and sniffs the sea squall, the moisture that goes right through your bones and corrodes your joints. The great writer's rheumatism...

In *Ulysses*, Leopold Bloom walks ten miles in a day — the same distance between the Martello tower and the National Library. More evidence for Max's idea that Joyce plotted his novel along his night run. But as for the marathon, James is enigmatic: — And Xenophon looked upon Marathon, Mr Dedalus said, looking again on the fireplace and to the window, and Marathon looked on the sea.

Is Irish stout, from the runner's perspective, nourishing or fattening? Does running make you age prematurely, or does it validate Zeno for all eternity by proving that Achilles never catches up with the tortoise? If Max weren't running, what would he be doing right now?

He passes a gaggle of kids, baseball caps backwards in best hip-hop style, who clap and cheer. The official photograph has already immortalized him. The German woman limped: like Joyce's Gertie, she ends up in a wheelchair.

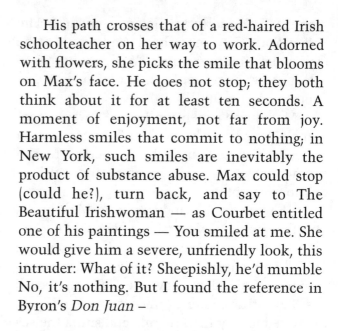

His path crosses that of a red-haired Irish schoolteacher on her way to work. Adorned with flowers, she picks the smile that blooms on Max's face. He does not stop; they both think about it for at least ten seconds. A moment of enjoyment, not far from joy. Harmless smiles that commit to nothing; in New York, such smiles are inevitably the product of substance abuse. Max could stop (could he?), turn back, and say to The Beautiful Irishwoman — as Courbet entitled one of his paintings — You smiled at me. She would give him a severe, unfriendly look, this intruder: What of it? Sheepishly, he'd mumble No, it's nothing. But I found the reference in Byron's *Don Juan* –

The mountains look on Marathon –
And Marathon looks on the sea;
And musing there an hour alone
I dream'd that Greece might yet be free.

* * *

Four miles from the finish line, the runners are in that zone where visions may come. Like Pheidippides, the runner of history's Marathon. Much has been made of him, most of it inaccurate: having run from Marathon to Athens with news of the victory over Darius, he is supposed to have fallen down dead after saying Rejoice! We triumph! Herodotus, a near-contemporary of the battle of Marathon who spoke to several eyewitnesses, provides a more exact account.

First, Pheidippides is a professional runner (*heremodromos*). He runs from Athens to Sparta, to deliver a plea for reinforcements, in a single day; that's about five times the distance of the modern marathon. At some stage he experiences a hallucinatory runner's high, for he claims to have encountered one of the gods. And he does not die.

Second, on September 13th of the year 490 B.C., the Athenians run into battle on the plain of Marathon — a martial arts first.

Third, nine thousand Athenians — not just Pheidippides — run the distance from Marathon to Athens, in order to reach their city before the Persians, who are in ships.

Fourth, the Spartan army has to run to reach Marathon in two days, for the distance they must cover is six times that of today's course.

The story involves a great many runners, in short. And no one dies from it, except for a few Athenian soldiers buried on Soros and the six thousand four hundred Persians under the tumuli. And probably not a single woman in the entire mêlée.

In fact, the *New England Journal of Medicine* cautions women against the heightened risk of osteoporosis, early menopause and symptoms identical to anorexia nervosa.

Marathon is, etymologically, the land by the sea, but the many places throughout the world that bear the same name do so in reference to the battle, a symbol of European resistance to the Iraqi-Iranian onslaught. There is a Marathon in Australia, another in Canada, and at least four in the United States (in Texas, Florida, Wisconsin and upstate New York). Marathon is even quoted on the stock exchange — it happens to be the name of a multinational oil company.

But legend is lovelier than reality. The runners now coming up to the last few miles are proud not to expire as they cross the finish line.

* * *

He crossed the border, like Gustave, deep inside the forest. From one jurisdiction to the next. If you were caught on one side for a crime committed on the other, it would slow down the procedure; you'd get significant mileage out of the small details that the cops overlooked in their haste to wrap things up quickly.

The tree-lined path, marked out for day-light rambling, was flat all the way to the abrupt zigzag that wound steeply up the slope. He leaned right, through the first hairpin, then left through the next, less than a hundred meters further on, where chalk peers out from dead leaves. After this Z, for Zorro, he crossed into the other territory, and felt a slight sense of satisfaction deep down in his belly: for the mission accomplished, the trick he's played on them. For revenge, consumed cold, on the blinkered lobby... And for a thousand other fantastic visions that only spurred him to go further and faster.

23
INTO CENTRAL PARK

> Levy crossed Columbus, picked up his pace a
> bit more as he closed in on Central Park, turned
> left at 95th, ran one block up and into the green
> area itself, straight to the tennis courts, and
> after that it was just a little half turn and then
> he was there.
> At the reservoir. [...]
> Levy easily passed other joggers as he began
> his initial circling of the water. It was half-past
> five — he always ran then, it was ideal for him.
>
> William Goldman, *Marathon Man*

Between 110th and 102nd, the blue line
hurtles down Fifth Avenue in its eager-
ness to reach Central Park. Then it turns right
and climbs, just for a few yards, just enough to
cut the ground from under your feet.
Outcroppings of natural stone appear: a raw,
dark granite.

The park (purchased for five and a half
million dollars in 1856) is one of the only
places in the city where nature reminds you
not to forget her. You half expect the Iroquois
to set up camp here and claim it as a reserva-
tion. Yet all is artifice: to create it, the land
was cleared in the last century of its poor,
their shanty towns and rubbish heaps. Today
it is larger than Monaco, but its eighty thousand trees still do not outnumber the homeless. For many New Yorkers, Central Park is

the only nature they will see anywhere other than on TV.

Now Max turns and runs backwards up the short slope, making best use of it in the manner prescribed in the book, The Blue Line. The Queensboro Bridge peeks out past the blocks of the Upper East Side. For Max, that was over an hour ago. The caravan of slower runners must still be crossing it, though Max can't make them out at this distance. Some (those over eighty, a few one-legged or otherwise severely handicapped participants) were given special permission to start the marathon at six o'clock this morning. The last among them will take more than twenty-two hours to complete the course, arriving at dawn tomorrow.

A banner across the road (NYCM — 23 MILES) reminds Max that, if he is to finish in under four hours, he has twenty-six minutes at his disposal. It will not be quite enough if he keeps to his average speed. Something sore, probably oozing blood, bursts in his foot. He knows from earlier practice sessions that he really needs twenty-nine minutes from this point.

In the early part of the century they added three hundred and eighty-five yards to the marathon so that it would finish under the royal box. If he were truly autonomous, he too would arbitrarily redraw the course, walk away from his walkman and Greenwar and air cargo terminals, and tell Ulysses to take a leap in the ocean. It takes only a slight incline to bring him down.

At the top of the rise the blue line turns left and meanders through the park for two miles, roughly parallel to Fifth Avenue, before emerging at the Plaza on the southeast corner. The blue line still attempts to hug each curve, but must now squeeze past throngs of spectators standing several rows deep along the whole of the final three-mile stretch, ready to cheer, comfort and, if necessary, evacuate.

The course cuts across the fourth of the park roads that are open to traffic. They've been designed so that the cars pass by below and almost out of sight, preserving the natural look. Max Frisch's carnivorous gray squirrels are in evidence. Though he would come and feed them here in peace and tranquillity, he still wrote: The writer does not retreat to an ivory tower but to a dynamite factory. Feltrinelli Editore?

In 1967 two women running under male pseudonyms were unmasked at the Boston marathon, the most selective in the US calendar. The ensuing scandal aided their cause, and everywhere the rules were rewritten to ensure the full participation of women, including those in wheelchairs.

And what if he had come across Ingeborg training in Central Park?

To the left is the park's center of gravity, a reservoir pinned onto the green expanse. Its waters stretch to within a few yards of the blue line; its one and a half miles of fencing serve as an infallible reference for those whose training is defined by a given number of circuits. More than a means of storing drinking water, it is the essential literary and cinematic backdrop. There are only two perspectives from which the spectator can be sure he or she is in New York: that of King Kong atop the Empire State Building and that of Dustin Hoffman, Marathon Man, running exhaustedly alongside the fence, with the Midtown skyline towering over trees and water in the background. And a sunset worthy of the seaside.

Those who have stopped to drink from this pool include Dos Passos, Hemingway, Truman Capote and Blaise Cendrars. Proust was almost alone in not coming here to dip his madeleine.

At the level of 90th Street, a spacious opening onto Fifth Avenue allows an appreciative glance at Frank Lloyd Wright's spiral, inside which Gustave is displayed on an inclined plane. Even at this late stage in the race, Max's thoughts turn to his calling, and before the Guggenheim he has mentally tipped his hat to the Cooper Hewitt, the Jewish Museum and the International Center of Photography.

The southern end of the reservoir goes slightly uphill and brings you to the back of the greenhouse which Kevin Roche designed for the Metropolitan Museum, almost as beautiful as his Ford Foundation Building on 42nd Street. When the French woman comes to see him, she takes him to the Met, to the four Courbets he loves: *Woman in the Waves, Woman with a Parrot, The Beautiful Irishwoman, Reclining Woman.*

Whereas the German woman never showed much interest in painting.

The blue line again tacks from one bend to another along its quasi-rural route. On a mound to the right, encircled by melancholy benches, an obelisk of red granite has been keeping watch over the Upper and Lower Kingdom since 1500 B.C, at a time when the Greeks were still pre-Olympic shepherds; its hieroglyphs praise the eternal line of the kings of Egypt.

Someone, a Frenchman who's run the Paris marathon a number of times, is comparing it to the Obélisque in the centre of the Place Concorde. He chats on remorselessly to his compatriot (by now speechless from exhaustion), saying the pink spire, one of Cleopatra's needles, is longer than his nose.

Further down, on a black marble plinth, the first Jagellon, King of Poland, commemorates the victory over the Teutonic Knights, on July 15th, 1410. And the blue line leaves the park circuit on April 23rd, 1864, the day Shakespeare's statue celebrated its model's 300th birthday, basking in the surrounding affection of all the plants mentioned in his plays.

On either side of the park live the aristocracy of the entertainment world. Living their lives in the public domain, they may, after the slightest domestic spat, take the kids and relocate to the west side of the park, then decide (with a little help from the Oscars) to move back to the east side. Or they may be assassinated, like John Lennon, while others are borne away to become an example for posterity.

* * *

To the west, he left behind a large farm that was also an inn. Under its vast gabled roof were gathered the cattle, the farmer's family and the Sunday customers who had come along to drink fermented cider. All asleep. There would have been a steaming board of smoked bacon and cream-cones for the children.

Patches of fog rising from the Rhine obscured the surrounding country, but happily it was straight and paved, and the snow had melted away. A sense of keen awareness remained, because of the lights down below, in Germany, on the other side of the misty river. Still straight, the road now began to climb, forcing the escapee to slow down. He was panting. A dog barked.

24
CENTRAL PARK EAST AND 84th STREET

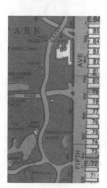

The column sets off at a brisk pace, and a blow from the butt of a rifle propels him ahead. The icy night air makes it hard for him to breathe. He lengthens his stride to put as much distance as possible between him and the S.S. trooper running beside him, on his left, panting like a bull. He glances at the S.S., whose face is twisted by a rictus. Maybe it's the effort, maybe the fact that he never stops screaming. Happily, he's not one of the S.S. with a dog. Suddenly, a sharp pain shoots through his right leg, and he realizes that he's barefoot. He must have hurt himself on some stone hidden in the muddy snow on the station platform. But he doesn't have time to worry about his feet. Instinctively, he tries to control his breathing, to adapt it to the rhythm of his stride. Suddenly he feels like laughing, he remembers the La Faisanderie stadium, the beautiful grass track among the spring trees.

Jorge Semprun, *The Cattle Truck*

The park is closed to traffic on weekends, as well as weekdays around noon, so that thousands of New Yorkers can get fit for the marathon or take breakfast at Tiffany's. People go there at night, too — perhaps to dream, or to be devoured by the long-toothed vampires, the Fisher King's hooded band, under a maple, an acacia or a ginkgo.

A triumphal arch of metal tubing, bedecked with sponsors' logos and the official time display, has graced the finish line for the past few days. There are eight rows of viewing stands on both sides of the finish, all the way down to the Columbus Circle entrance, then a jumble of satellite dishes, tightrope-walking cameramen setting up for overhead shots, hundreds and hundreds of buses, pre-fabs lifted in by helicopter, luxury Conestogas gaudier than any circus ringmaster's. The wagon train stretches across the vast prairie, as far as the eye can see. Police watch; security guards guard. The curious have been coming since Wednesday to have their photos taken in front of the official stands, arms in the air, throwing kisses to crowds in absentia, trying out the arrival lanes, where some will receive medals, everyone will be given a thermal poncho and each female marathoner will be handed a red rose.

But no, there is no coup de théâtre, and not a single mile is awarded free of charge. Phileas Fogg is not there to give you a discount on an extra time zone.

Baron Pierre de Coubertin came up with the idea of the modern Olympics when asked by the government to undertake a reform of physical education in French schools. The games were reborn in Athens, in 1896.

That same year, on September 20th, the first New York marathon was organized by the Knickerbocker Athletic Club. Thirty runners made it to Columbia Oval, led by John J. McDermott, who finished in three hours and twenty-five minutes. The medical advice and sports wisdom of that era would have been quite different from those any reader can find today in Max's book, *The Blue Line*, on page 171.

It is a race against the clock. Max starts to notice familiar faces around him, run-

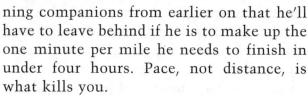

ning companions from earlier on that he'll have to leave behind if he is to make up the one minute per mile he needs to finish in under four hours. Pace, not distance, is what kills you.

He arranges for his memory to be unfaithful, erasing all the miles from his mind except those ahead. If he wrote a book, he would call it *Everybody Has Two Names,* in order to emphasize the morality of ambiguity (another title, already spoken for). His inability to refer to himself in the first person singular is proverbial. Max and his double, at all times. In the middle of this cheering crowd and under these trees, his personae are about to come together. The architect, a Frenchman from a well-to-do family... a Khmer Vert... a man running the New York marathon.

Take care of yourself, Max says to himself, you only have one.

Ingeborg fought the lobby in solitary. The Swiss modus operandi, that's what the cops called it; it was her best hope of escaping capture. Her wheelchair could well conceal a mission control center. Disability as ideological camouflage.

Run, Max, run. Your past is in front of you.

* * *

Through the wooded terrain, the open road remained calm. Not so the fugitive, who increased his pace without taking his eyes off the pinpoints of light nestling in the valley to his right. They might have heard the explosion in the hamlet below — but it might have been muffled by the topography. Was the mountain opposite more likely to have absorbed the sound or projected it back? Did some insomniac get up to take a look, let his dogs out to have a sniff around?

By following an arc along the ridge, he would certainly not be seen by the villagers, but against vehicles he would be defenseless. For now, there were no headlight beams sweeping the landscape and no dogs barking. He stopped at the point where the dirt road became a paved one, took the black pepper out of his pocket, and scattered it. A delaying tactic. The police dogs would stop here too, and their masters would decree that the fugitive must have been picked up by an accomplice in a vehicle. Down in the hamlet, someone would eventually be found who thought he remembered hearing a car at, yes, around three in the morning. The rumor would be taken up and amplified by the media.

He slipped the pepper-cone in his pocket and set off, on foot, with renewed zest.

25
CENTRAL PARK EAST
AND 66th STREET

First it [the Dodo] marked out a race-course, in
a sort of circle, ("the exact shape doesn't matter," it said,) and then all the party were placed
along the course, here and there. There was no
"One, two, three, and away," but they began
running when they liked, and left off when
they liked, so that it was not easy to know
when the race was over. However, when they
had been running half an hour or so, and were
quite dry again, the Dodo suddenly called out
"The race is over!" and they all crowded round
it, panting, and asking, "But who has won?"

Lewis Carroll,
Alice's Adventures in Wonderland

W
here 66th Street would be if it crossed
the park, a double line marked NYCM
— 25 MILES is crowned with balloons and
strewn with the last paper cups. The official
photograph now: smile, you've been captured on film, for a souvenir that you can
purchase when they contact you at home in
a few weeks. It shows the many states of
physical decay on view from here on in.
There are those unable to lift off at all, legs
heavy with foul blood, and others whose
stride has shortened by half or whose hands
flap uselessly at shoulder height. Counting
every step, saving one last deathly grin for
the finish. Their running is slower than

walking, their walk is more torturous than your love affairs. Say cheese!

Max smiles for the photo, but too soon. He floats, gripping his thumbs in his fists. Nobody's passing him at this point, but one in every ten or so falters and drops behind.

On the right is the zoo, with its long vowel like a diphthong, and to the left The Pond, with its capital letters.

What the German woman wants from him is, to his delight, more explosive than dynamite. Confidential information. Revealed, the military aircraft for which the landing strip and cargo bays have been specifically designed; revealed, the names of the Japanese investors trying to conceal their involvement. Is that what they mean by acting with impunity?

There was the hollow decade of the Eighties, all cynicism and no future, when activism was roundly mocked and reality could only be referred to within at least three pairs of quotation marks. Now comes the return of realism. Time to describe, to testify. With irony, if required for the sake of a fuller understanding. Things must be named. That tree is a ginkgo, and that one, with its yellowing autumn leaves, is an acacia. Without reference to the memory of a photograph, glimpsed in a mirror, of a tree that evoked (for one Japanese writer) the existential venom of the ginkgo.

Are you for the lobby, or against it? Radiation sickness is not an expression of the intangible morbidity of virtual time. Keep your feet on the ground, Max.

Leaning sharply into a left-hand bend, as required by the blue line, Max leaves the southeast corner of the park and heads into Grand Army Plaza. And which Grand Army might that be? The Red? Napoleon's? Alexander's? The one led by Hippias at

Marathon, or the one that fought in the Gulf? No time to answer, for the applause from the balconies of the Plaza Hotel (elderly ladies in their fur coats, makeup and gloves, their cigar-smoking chauffeurs) is meant for him. His run is bathed in a state of grace, free of care. An ecstatic distance.

On this autumn Sunday afternoon, Gustave has set up his easel in a dark studio whose only window looks out on Central Park. Possibly the suite that Frank Lloyd Wright rented at the Plaza — all enclosed spaces are alike. From his palette he adds blue touches to the sky over Ornans. The painter has put himself at the center of the painting. The model for the Irishwoman is pulling a sheet up over her bare breasts. On the left, the common people in all their shapes and sizes. On the right, his friends: Proudhon, reciting the catechism in his sleep; Baudelaire, engrossed in a book of reproductions; Max Buchon, who made his way secretly to Switzerland with the help of Courbet's family. Next to the window, two lovers in a tender embrace, indifferent to the cheers of the crowd all around the park. At the far end of the studio are extracts from the artist's work (women bathing, woman with red hair); in the center, his work in progress: the leaf-fringed Loue, the chalky outcroppings of the Jura, a glint of playful trout.

As a child, Max would trap fish with his mother's nylon stockings. At fifteen, he used dynamite to burst their gills underwater, a method banned for its cruelty.

Why aren't they outside, posing in the open air? *Le déjeûner sur l'herbe* in Central Park, the men in their dark suits, autumn on the skin of the nude Irishwoman. I'm fucking a servant, Gustave wrote to his friend, my wife being a married woman.

Whatever the season, whatever the angle of the sun at any given point on the planet, Max's tan endures. It takes readily to his skin and crumples it with age, a defiant reminder. You see? I'm still in touch with life. Not the life of offices, subways and bedrooms, but the one I act out in the open air of solitary paths and the close air of cities and barricades. Real life is outside. As the other Gustave says, almost simultaneously, Rioting is the only politics I understand.

Courbet is painting, from memory, the blue of a Jura sky, at the very spot on the canvas where Max knows he must break the line, call out from the street and its rumbling marathon.

Still in his shorts and singlet, he bounds into the Plaza — the doormen too astonished to react — and goes up to the third floor. Sweat dripping on the thick pile, he breaks down the door with his shoulder, shouting, Gustave, we have to talk!

Not now, says the painter. Can't you see I'm filming the scene of my life? It's an interior, all my friends are here. We're launching a manifesto, the New Activism.

Yes, says Max, so am I. But I only like exteriors. Ingeborg is pursuing me, I don't know what to tell her.

Tell her yes, orders Gustave.

With a flourish, he paints a line of blue across his glasses.

To bring him back down to earth.

* * *

Still running, he burst through the foliage onto the path, using his shoulder. Frauenwald, the Forest of Women, a stand of broad-leaved trees on the other side of the highway. The kind of name people remembered. Where the

path split in three, he took the middle way, which led to a place simply called Berg (mountain). It took a few minutes to negotiate the three uphill curves that brought him a hundred meters higher.

His eardrums still reverberated with the explosive force of several kilograms of Nobel's jelly. For a just cause, my lords of the lobby. The movement of his forehead, rising a few centimeters with each stride, made the beam cast by the headlamp dance forwards and back along the path. His whole body was shaking; certain muscles seemed to have locked permanently; they would never carry him the full forty-two kilometers through the night to save his skin.

He glanced anxiously at the chronometer, which showed less than ten minutes, and tried to regulate his breathing as the next junction — another path up from the Rhine — approached. From there, according to his book:

A backward glance reveals the Black. Forest and the heights of Dinkelberg and Hotzenwald. At the next intersection (point 415) follow the narrow path along the edge of the forest as far as Schönenberg (point 468). Cross the meadow until you reach a farm (Schönenbuel), then continue on the other side of the Magden-to-Olsberg road towards another farm (Dorn, point 462). From there, it is a straight uphill climb to the forest. The first section is very steep and leads to Girspel. The border is reached soon thereafter via a path that runs alongside a wide gully. A milestone marks the actual frontier (point 571). Take the right-hand path out of the forest and continue up the

Dumberg face to the village of Hersberg. Leaving the village, the path to the Schword Forest is signposted.

Letting the book (which he knew by heart) guide his steps, he switched off the miner's lamp on his forehead.

26
CENTRAL PARK WEST AND 62nd STREET

At the Plaza Hotel, the final turn into the finish, on a rise. A relief, but the end was not yet in sight. As we drew nearer we urged each other on. The yellow-coated volunteers congratulated us individually: "Wonderful, pretty, oh man, lovely, oh girl, wonderful, marvelous!" Each of us received a medal and a Xeroxed certificate.

Through the misty park and its hidden paths it came, returning from its battle against Alexander: an army of weary and silent foot soldiers, now cloaked in thin silvery capes to ward off the chill, the vibrant wail of exhaustion echoing all around.

Günter Herburger, *Lauf und Wahn*

After the Plaza, it runs along the south side of the park to Columbus Circle on the west corner, then dives back into the artificial nature. Ginkgo-side, the fans stand many rows deep, and city-side they overflow along both perpendiculars, Sixth Avenue — named for the Americas — and Seventh. There is not enough strength left in the Athenian foot soldiers for them to turn their heads in the direction of the cheers cascading from the windows. The hotels have grown straight and tall to get a better view of the green: after Gustave's, there is the Park Lane, the St. Moritz, the Barbizon Plaza, the Navarro and the Marriott Essex, whose sign can be plainly seen from the reservoir.

What the German woman has in mind is, if anything, worse than an armed attack: to expose the lobby's intrigues to the light of day.

At Columbus Circle, where Eighth picks up again, a giant screen relays every twist and dramatic turn in the race. TV coverage will be continuous until the last runner crosses the finish line. The camera zooms in from a low angle for a close-up of rows of shoes rising, falling. Impossible for the runners to avoid seeing themselves, blown up to a height of four stories, as they run. An image of reality beyond the virtual, this is the media's latest inspiring gesture.

At the top of the screen is a time display that Ingeborg (who, Max suspects, is in Nagasaki, at breakfast-time) can also see. She speaks into his headset:

"Where are you, Max?"

But he knows she's figured it out for him. She knows where he is. A few strides away from the finish, and a decision that has ripened with each passing mile.

He wants to be the one somebody leans on. His legs and lungs have not given way. He has even broken through the Wall. But the Max now arriving is another one: Max the magnificent.

Under the paving stones, they promised the beach. What you find there is in fact the underground, a subway with or without graffiti that may or may not be running — impossible to guess, unless you see the passengers emerging in successive waves. Max is running both above and below the surface. He brings the microphone to his lips; his voice flies up to the satellite and beams down on the German woman.

"You can count on me."

"Max, leave your mike open. I want you live."

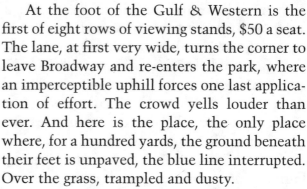

At the foot of the Gulf & Western is the first of eight rows of viewing stands, $50 a seat. The lane, at first very wide, turns the corner to leave Broadway and re-enters the park, where an imperceptible uphill forces one last application of effort. The crowd yells louder than ever. And here is the place, the only place where, for a hundred yards, the ground beneath their feet is unpaved, the blue line interrupted. Over the grass, trampled and dusty.

A few years ago, as the leading pack of five was coming through, a strong gust of wind lifted the dust and debris into a whirlwind that blinded and choked them without warning. The film shows what happens as they emerge from the dust cloud: one is running backwards, another is going in the wrong direction, a third covers his face with his hands, and one has actually fallen. A lone Kenyan — used to the sandstorms of the savanna — steals a twenty-yard advantage on the rest and wins the contest. The third world triumphant in the middle of New York City.

This year no such mishap will spoil the end of the ordeal: wire mesh has been laid over the turf to guard against dust, or puddles left by a passing rainstorm.

The line begins again immediately afterwards. The — blue — line –ah. Three breaths out, one in. The, blue, line, ah...

* * *

He placed the container on top of the gate on the second floor of the building, over the central staircase. At least two meters of fuse hung out, the almost instantaneous kind. Then slow pyrotechnic fuse that burns at five centimeters per minute. Times five. He hasn't miscalculated: ten times five equals half a meter, which makes ten minutes.

Isn't that right, Giangi?

He could feel the perspiration inside the surgical gloves, despite the talc. He took out a lighter, used it, returned it to his pocket –consciously depriving the lobby of a piece of evidence — and started the chronometer.

Click.

A quick glance outside towards the spot where the night watchman, in exactly thirty minutes, would find the warning sign.

Down the stairs, keeping his head bowed because of the light on his forehead. Deliberately and slowly, in spite of the countdown initiated by the flame. A bad fall in the next twenty meters and he would go up with the whole place. He hoisted one leg gently across a window ledge, and stiffened. Fear and excitement hammering him. Pulled the other leg over, caught his pants on something. Unhooked it. No, it was nothing. Went around the fence, his back to the building, headed towards the forest. Turned off the headlamp. Knew (having gone over it so often in his mind) that three minutes had elapsed and two remained.

A service tunnel under the highway. Thanks to countless blind rehearsals, he found it instantly. Bending over so as not to hit his head. Not sure whether to cover his ears yet. Out the other side, into the shelter of the woods.

It was called *Zabriskie Point*, by Antonioni. That long, suffocating detonation. Exploded fragments in slow motion in the sky, across the screen. A blast more muffled and more long-lasting than he had expected, like the far-off echo of the starting cannon, at the Verrazano Toll Plaza.

He wept for joy. Max weeps for joy.

Succeeded. Max succeeds.

Le souffle,
au pied poudreux — de l'un à l'autre,
clairsemé.

André du Bouchet,
Dans la chaleur vacante

About the Author

Daniel de Roulet was born in Switzerland in 1944. A writer, architect and information worker, he is the author of the following works in French:

A nous deux, Ferdinand, Canevas Editeur, 1991 (Bourse de la Commission littéraire de langue française du canton de Berne, New York 1992.)

Virtuellement vôtre, Canevas Editeur, 1993 (Prix Dentan, 1994).

La vie, il y a des enfants pour ça, Canevas Editeur, 1994.

La ligne bleue, Le Seuil, 1995 (Babet d'Or de Lettres Frontières, Saint-Etienne, 1995; Sélection Prix Renaudot, 1995; Prix de Littérature Alpes-Jura, Paris, 1996.)

Bleu Siècle, Le Seuil, 1996 (Bourse de Pro Helvetia, 1996; Résidence de la Fondation Landis et Gyr, London 1998).

Double, Canevas Editeur, 1998 (Prix Pittard de l'Andelyn, 1999; Grand Prix de Littérature du Canton de Berne, 1999).

Gris-bleu, Le Seuil, 1999.

Courir, écrire, Minizoè, 2000.

The Blue Line is his first novel published in English translation.

AUTONOMEDIA BOOK SERIES

MARX BEYOND MARX
Lessons on the Gründrisse
Antonio Negri $12

MAGPIE REVERIES
James Koehnline $12

SCANDAL
Essays in Islamic Heresy
Peter Lamborn Wilson $12

TROTSKYISM AND MAOISM
Theory & Practice in France & the U.S.
A. Belden Fields $12

ON ANARCHY & SCHIZOANALYSIS
Rolando Perez $10

FILE UNDER POPULAR
Theoretical & Critical Writing on Music
Chris Cutler $10

RETHINKING MARXISM
Steve Resnick & Rick Wolff, eds. $12

THE DAMNED UNIVERSE
OF CHARLES FORT
Louis Kaplan, ed. $10

CLIPPED COINS, ABUSED WORDS,
CIVIL GOVERNMENT
John Locke's Philosophy of Money
Constantine George Caffentzis $10

HORSEXE
Essay on Transsexuality
Catherine Millot $12

THE DAUGHTER
Roberta Allen $8

GULLIVER
Michael Ryan $7

THE NARRATIVE BODY
Eldon Garnet $10

MEDIA ARCHIVE
*Foundation for the Advancement
of Illegal Knowledge* $14

THE NEW ENCLOSURES
Midnight Notes Collective $6

GOD AND PLASTIC SURGERY
Marx, Nietzsche, Freud & the Obvious
Jeremy Barris $12

MODEL CHILDREN
Inside the Republic of Red Scarves
Paul Thorez $10

COLUMBUS & OTHER CANNIBALS
The Wétiko Disease & The White Man
Jack Forbes $12

A DAY IN THE LIFE
Tales from the Lower East Side
Alan Moore & Josh Gosniak, eds. $12

CASSETTE MYTHOS
The New Music Underground
Robin James, ed. $12

ENRAGÉS & SITUATIONISTS
The Occupation Movement, May '68
René Viénet $12

MIDNIGHT OIL
Work, Energy, War, 1973–1992
Midnight Notes Collective $10

GONE TO CROATAN
Origins of North American Dropout Culture
James Koehnline & Ron Sakolsky, eds. $14

ABOUT FACE
Race in Postmodern America
Timothy Maliqalim Simone $12

THE ARCANE OF REPRODUCTION
Housework, Prostitution, Labor & Capital
Leopoldina Fortunati $10

BY ANY MEANS NECESSARY
Outlaw Manifestos & Ephemera, 1965–70
Peter Stansill & David Mairowitz, eds. $14

FORMAT AND ANXIETY
Collected Essays on the Media
Paul Goodman $12

FILM AND POLITICS
IN THE THIRD WORLD
John Downing, ed. $12

DEMONO (THE BOXED GAME)
P.M. $11.95

AUTONOMEDIA   PO BOX 568, WILLIAMSBURGH STATION   BROOKLYN NY 11211
INFO@AUTONOMEDIA.ORG   WWW.AUTONOMEDIA.ORG   TEL/FAX 718 963-2603

AUTONOMEDIA BOOK SERIES

WILD CHILDREN
David Mandl & Peter Lamborn Wilson., eds.   *$5*

¡ZAPATISTAS!
Documents of the New Mexican Revolution
EZLN $12

THE OFFICIAL KGB HANDBOOK
USSR Committee for State Security $12

CRIMES OF THE BEATS
The Unbearables $12

AN EXISTING BETTER WORLD
Notes on the Bread and Puppet Theatre
George Dennison $14

CARNIVAL OF CHAOS
On the Road with the Nomadic Festival
Sascha Altman Dubrul $8

DREAMER OF THE DAY
Francis Parker Yockey & the
Postwar Fascist Underground
Kevin Coogan $15.95

THE ANARCHISTS
A Portrait of Civilization at the
End of the 19th Century
John Henry Mackay $12

POLITICAL ESSAYS
Richard Kostelanetz $14

ESCAPE FROM THE
NINETEENTH CENTURY
Essays on Marx, Fourier, Proudhon & Nietzsche
Peter Lamborn Wilson $12

THE UNBEARABLES ANTHOLOGY
The Unbearables $12

BLOOD & VOLTS
Tesla, Edison, and the Electric Chair
Th. Metzger $12

PIONEER OF INNER SPACE
The Life of Fitz Hugh Ludlow
Donald P. Dulchinos $14

CHRON!IC!RIOTS!PA!SM!
Fly $8

PSYCHEDELICS REIMAGINED
Introduced by Timothy Leary,
Prefaced by Hakim Bey
Tom Lyttle, Editor $14

ROTTING GODDESS
The Origin of the Witch in Classical Antiquity
Jacob Rabinowitz $12

THE IBOGAINE STORY
The Staten Island Project
Paul Di Rienzo & Dana Beal $15

BLUE TIDE
The Search for Soma
Mike Jay $14

THE BLUE LINE
Daniel de Roulet $12

TEACH YOURSELF FUCKING
Tuli Kupferberg $15

CALIBAN & THE WITCHES
Silvia Federici $14

READ ME!
ASCII Culture and the Revenge of Knowledge
Nettime $18

SOUNDING OFF!
Music as Subversion/Resistance/Revolution
Fred Ho & Ron Sakolsky, Editors $15

AGAINST THE MEGAMACHINE
Essays on Empire and its Enemies
David Watson $14

BEYOND BOOKCHIN
Preface for a Future Social Ecology
David Watson $8

WAR IN THE NEIGHBORHOOD
Seth Tobocman $20

NIGHT VISION
Libretto & Double Audio CD
Fred Ho & Ruth Margraff $20

CONVERSATIONS WITH DON DURITO
Stories of the Defeat of Neo–Liberalism
EZLN Subcomandante Insurgente Marcos $12

AUTONOMEDIA   PO BOX 568, WILLIAMSBURGH STATION   BROOKLYN NY 11211
INFO@AUTONOMEDIA.ORG   WWW.AUTONOMEDIA.ORG   TEL/FAX 718 963-2603

AUTONOMEDIA BOOK SERIES

AURORAS OF THE ZAPATISTAS
Midnight Notes $14

DIGITAL RESISTANCE
Critical Art Ensemble $12

EXTENDED MEDIA OBJECT
Vladimir Muzesky, ed. $18

THE FORECAST IS HOT!
Surrealist Subversion in Chicago
Ron Sakolsky, ed. $15

GRASS
Ron Mann $20

HACKTIVISM
Electronic Disturbance Theatre $15

FORBIDDEN SACRAMENTS
The Shamanic Tradition in Western Civilization
Donald P. Dulchinos $14

HELP YOURSELF!
The Unbearables $14

I'M STILL THINKING
Art from the Balkan Wars
Miro Stefanovic $12

NIETZSCHE & ANARCHISM
John Moore, ed. $14

LAB U.S.A.
Illuminated Documents
Kevin Pyle $14

AUTONOMEDIA DISTRIBUTION

DRUNKEN BOAT
An Anarchist Review of Literature
and the Arts
Max Blechman, ed. $7

LUSITANIA
A Journal of Reflection & Oceanography
Martim Avillez, ed.

FELIX
The Review of Television & Video Culture
Kathy High, ed.

RACE TRAITOR
A Journal of the New Abolitionism
John Garvey & Noel Ignatiev, eds.

FRUIT
Anne D'Adesky, ed.

BENEATH THE EMPIRE OF THE BIRDS
Carl Watson $13

BLACK MASK AND UP AGAINST THE
WALL MOTHERFUCKER
Ron Hahne $10

LIVING IN VOLKSWAGEN BUSES
Julian Beck $12.95

I SHOT MUSSOLINI
Elden Garnet $14.95

ANARCHY AFTER LEFTISM
Bob Black $6.95

ALL COTTON BRIEFS
M. Kasper $8

BELLE CATASTROPHE
Carl Watson & Shalom $14.95

ELEMENTS OF REFUSAL
John Zerzan $14.95

MORE AND LESS
Sylvère Lotringer, ed. $14

THE CONGRESS OF CLOWNS
Joel Schechter $10

I AM SECRETLY AN IMPORTANT MAN
Steven Jesse Bernstein $12.95

BRICOLAGE EX MACHINA
Carl Watson $10

BEEN THERE AND BACK TO NOWHERE
Ursula Biemann $30

AUTONOMEDIA   PO BOX 568, WILLIAMSBURGH STATION   BROOKLYN NY 11211
INFO@AUTONOMEDIA.ORG   WWW.AUTONOMEDIA.ORG   TEL/FAX 718 963-2603

AUTONOMEDIA NEW AUTONOMY SERIES

Jim Fleming & Peter Lamborn Wilson, Editors

BETWEEN DOG AND WOLF
Essays on Art & Politics
David Levi Strauss $8

T.A.Z.
The Temporary Autonomous Zone
Hakim Bey $8

THIS IS YOUR FINAL WARNING!
Thom Metzger $8

FRIENDLY FIRE
Bob Black $7

FIRST AND LAST EMPERORS
The Absolute State and The Body of the Despot
Kenneth Dean & Brian Massumi $7

SHOWER OF STARS
The Initiatic Dream in Sufism & Taoism
Peter Lamborn Wilson $8

THIS WORLD WE MUST LEAVE
AND OTHER ESSAYS
Jacques Camatte $8

PIRATE UTOPIAS
Moorish Corsairs & European Renegadoes
Peter Lamborn Wilson $8

40TH CENTURY MAN
Andy Clausen $8

FLESH MACHINE
Cyborgs, Designer Babies & the
New Eugenic Consciousness
Critical Art Ensemble $8

THE ELECTRONIC DISTURBANCE
Critical Art Ensemble $7

X TEXTS
Derek Pell $7

POLEMICS
Jack Collom, Anselm Hollo, Anne Waldman $8

WIGGLING WISHBONE
Stories of Patasexual Speculation
Bart Plantenga $7

FUTURE PRIMITIVE & OTHER ESSAYS
John Zerzan $7

WHORE CARNIVAL
Shannon Bell, ed. $8

CRIMES OF CULTURE
Richard Kostelanetz $7

INVISIBLE GOVERNANCE
The Art of African Micropolitics
David Hecht & Maliqalim Simone $8

THE LIZARD CLUB
Steve Abbott $7

CRACKING THE MOVEMENT
Squatting Beyond the Media
*Foundation for the Advancement
of Illegal Knowledge $7*

SOCIAL OVERLOAD
Henri-Pierre Jeudy $7

ELECTRONIC CIVIL DISOBEDIENCE
Critical Arts Ensemble $8

THE TOUCH
Michael Brownstein $7

MILLENNIUM
Hakim Bey $8

AVANT GARDENING
P. Lamborn Wilson & Bill Weinberg, eds. $8

CAUGHT LOOKING
Feminism, Pornography & Censorship
Feminist Anti-Censorship Taskforce $15.95

DOCTOR PENETRALIA
Th. Metzger $14

AUTONOMEDIA CALENDARS

THE AUTONOMEDIA CALENDAR
OF JUBILEE SAINTS
James Koehnline & Autonomedia Collective $8

THE SHEROES AND
WOMYN WARRIORS CALENDAR
O.R.S.S.A.S.M. $8

AUTONOMEDIA   PO BOX 568, WILLIAMSBURGH STATION   BROOKLYN NY 11211
INFO@AUTONOMEDIA.ORG   WWW.AUTONOMEDIA.ORG   TEL/FAX 718 963-2603

BLACK & RED PRESS

AGAINST HIS-STORY,
AGAINST LEVIATHAN!
Fredy Perlman $5

BOLSHEVIKS & WORKERS' CONTROL
The State and Counter-Revolution
Maurice Brinton $2.50

HAVING LITTLE, BEING MUCH
A Chronicle of Fredy Perlman's Fifty Years
Lorraine Perlman $3.50

MOMENTOS
Compendio Poetico
Federico Arcos $1

HUNGARY '56
Andy Anderson $2.50

THE CONTINUING APPEAL
OF NATIONALISM
Fredy Perlman $1.50

LETTERS OF INSURGENTS
Sophia Nachalo and Yarostan Vochek $7.50

LIP AND THE SELF-MANAGED
COUNTER-REVOLUTION
Négation $1.75

OBJECTIVITY AND LIBERAL
SCHOLARSHIP
Noam Chomsky $6

PLUNDER: A PLAY
Fredy Perlman $2

POLAND, 1980-1982
Class Struggle and the Crisis of Capital
Henri Simon $2.50

POVERTY OF STUDENT LIFE
Situationist International $4

THE REPRODUCTION OF EVERYDAY LIFE
Fredy Perlman $1

SOCIETY OF THE SPECTACLE
Guy Debord $6

THE STORY OF TATIANA
Jacques Baynac $6

THE STRAIT
Fredy Perlman $6

THE WANDERING OF HUMANITY
Jacques Camatte $1.25

FLY BY NIGHT PRESS
Steve Cannon, Editor

SKULLS HEAD SAMBA
Eve Packer $8

WATERWORN
Star Black $10

PAGAN OPERETTA
Carl Hancock Rux $14.95

SKYSCRAPERS, TAXIS AND TAMPONS
Poetry by Seven Young NYC Women *$10.95*

BROKEN NOSES AND METEMPSYCHOSES
Michael Carter $10

Ordering Information
Please send check or money order, payable to Autonomedia, to the address below.
Credit card orders can be made by website, telephone, fax, or email.

Shipping Charges
Please include US $3.00 for the first book, and Us $1.00 per each additional title.
All books are shipped UPS or by first class mail, unless otherwise specified.

AUTONOMEDIA   PO BOX 568, WILLIAMSBURGH STATION   BROOKLYN NY 11211
INFO@AUTONOMEDIA.ORG   WWW.AUTONOMEDIA.ORG   TEL/FAX 718 963-2603 .